THE FIRST THOUSAND TREES

ALSO BY PREMEE MOHAMED

IN THIS SERIES

The Annual Migration of Clouds

We Speak Through the Mountain

NOVELS

Beneath the Rising

A Broken Darkness

The Void Ascendant

The Siege of Burning Grass

COLLECTIONS

No One Will Come Back for Us and Other Stories

One Message Remains

NOVELLAS

The Butcher of the Forest

And What Can We Offer You Tonight

These Lifeless Things

The Apple-Tree Throne

The Rider, The Ride, The Rich Man's Wife

PREMEE MOHAMED

THE FIRST THOUSAND TREES

ECW

Copyright © Premee Mohamed, 2025

Published by ECW Press
665 Gerrard Street East
Toronto, Ontario, Canada M4M 1Y2
416-694-3348 / info@ecwpress.com

All rights reserved. No part of this publication may be reproduced, stored in a retrieval system, or transmitted in any form by any process — electronic, mechanical, photocopying, recording, or otherwise — without the prior written permission of the copyright owners and ECW Press. The scanning, uploading, and distribution of this book via the Internet or via any other means without the permission of the publisher is illegal and punishable by law. This book may not be used for text and data mining, AI training, and similar technologies. Please purchase only authorized electronic editions, and do not participate in or encourage electronic piracy of copyrighted materials. Your support of the author's rights is appreciated.

Editor for the Press: Jen R. Albert
Copy editor: Rachel Ironstone
Cover and interior illustrations: Veronica Park
Cover design: Jess Albert

This is a work of fiction. Names, characters, places, and incidents either are the product of the author's imagination or are used fictitiously, and any resemblance to actual persons, living or dead, business establishments, events, or locales is entirely coincidental.

Library and Archives Canada Cataloguing in Publication

Title: The first thousand trees / Premee Mohamed.

Names: Mohamed, Premee, author

Description: Series statement: The annual migration of clouds series ; 3

Identifiers: Canadiana (print) 20250215098 | Canadiana (ebook) 20250215101

ISBN 978-1-77041-734-2 (softcover)
ISBN 978-1-77852-390-8 (ePub)
ISBN 978-1-77852-391-5 (PDF)

Subjects: LCGFT: Dystopian fiction. | LCGFT: Novellas.

Classification: LCC PS8626.O44735 F57 2025 | DDC C813/.6—dc23

This book is funded in part by the Government of Canada. Ce livre est financé en partie par le gouvernement du Canada. We acknowledge the support of the Canada Council for the Arts. Nous remercions le Conseil des arts du Canada de son soutien. We acknowledge the funding support of the Ontario Arts Council (OAC), an agency of the Government of Ontario. We also acknowledge the support of the Government of Ontario through the Ontario Book Publishing Tax Credit, and through Ontario Creates. We acknowledge the support of the Province of Alberta through Alberta Foundation for the Arts.

Canada

Canada Council for the Arts Conseil des arts du Canada

Ontario

ONTARIO ARTS COUNCIL
CONSEIL DES ARTS DE L'ONTARIO
an Ontario government agency
un organisme du gouvernement de l'Ontario

ONTARIO CREATES

Alberta Foundation for the Arts

PRINTED AND BOUND IN CANADA

PRINTING: FRIESENS 5 4 3 2 1

Get the ebook free!*
*proof of purchase required

Purchase the print edition and receive the ebook free.
For details, go to ecwpress.com/ebook.

For Kim

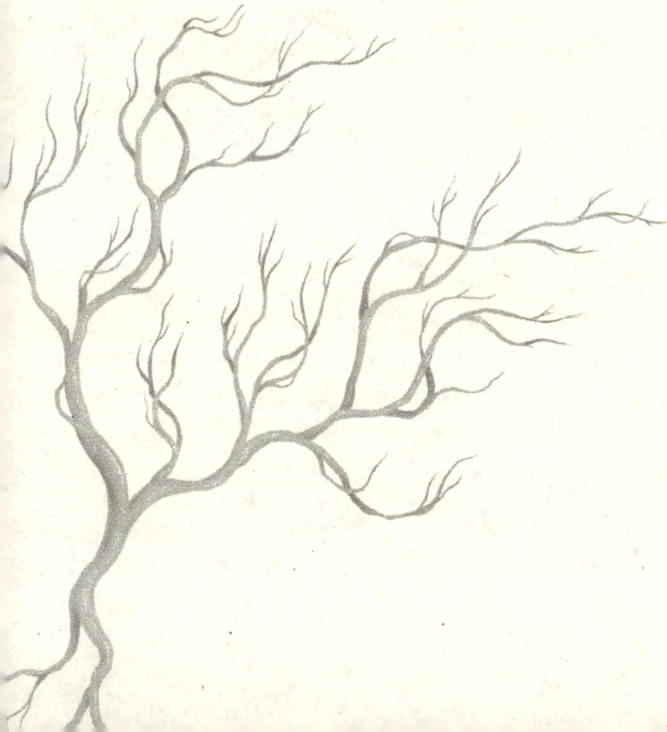

1.

From the moment humanity conceived of gods, we came up with their great punishment: divine transformation. Supposedly, I should say. Allegedly. If you had angered a deity, maybe it would flog or crush or hang or eat you, give you a never-ending and ever-renewing task, blast your lands, blight your crops, strike barren any nearby wombs; or maybe it would say, *You are changed.*

Man into stag (torn apart). Nymph into pillar of stone (as one does). Man into pine tree. Girl into beautiful white heifer. Or spider or tortoise or mountain or river. Or a *monster* . . .

"What do I have to do," I prayed as I walked. "Tell me. Anything. I'll do it. Only make me a monster too." I didn't even know what I was praying to, or why one would pray to it for punishment. In my head, every god I'd ever heard of joined some vast disorganized pantheon that never shrank, only expanded, as I thought of additions.

That rock I saw yesterday: a god.

Then at night, the raven studying me as I ate: a god.

Today: I woke to the smell of smoke, but I saw clearly and the sun was unobstructed. The presence of a god, the tracks of a god. Theosophical ichnology.

I left a place that did not give a single shit about me and I am searching for a place that might be the same. I hope not. But at least (I tell myself) I will come as a prophet out of the wilderness, because I am unannounced. And a little bit unhinged. It's been a long walk.

In the distance, a dog began to bark — a big dog or a dog practised at sounding big. Short proud chestful booms echoing like falling masonry. The dog had a message for me. The dog said: I know you are coming.

Hmm. Announced after all.

They came to meet me when my map said I was still hours away. One dog, one man. The dog was even bigger than I had feared — eighty or ninety pounds, camouflaged with thick fur the colour of the burned forest, all char-white and ash-grey and charcoal-black. No collar, no leash. Even before I realized that it was loose, my heart was hammering hard enough to make me lightheaded. Everyone said they can smell fear. Would it attack at the smell? Was it *trained* to attack?

The man was so lean he looked like he did not outweigh his animal. As I approached he seemed to vibrate with impatience, but he did not walk to meet me. Not that there was a protocol or ceremony but that I was the supplicant, I should know my place, I must come to *him*. His hands were empty and that surprised me, but I supposed he didn't need to threaten me with a weapon if he had an animal he could control.

Closer to, I saw he *was* armed — a wrist-thick spear strapped across his back, the stone point rising a full foot above his shoulder. The moment I knew what it was I turned my hands palm out, showing him I held nothing. Out here it did not signify some unbreakable chivalric rule, of course; but it had gotten me this far.

"What do you want?" the man said when we were close enough to talk.

"I'm headed to Sprucedown," I said.

"The fuck you are."

In my startled silence, the dog growled, a murmur I felt through the soles of my shoes. I resisted a brief but sickening urge to turn and run, and only managed to restrain myself with the mental image of what would happen if the dog reacted badly to sudden movements. For just a moment I felt again the terrible enormity of the world that overtook me when I least wanted it: the thousands of miles of empty landscape around us, the crumbling road on which we now stood, the punishing sun that did not care about the lack of shade, and the fact that I could be killed here — or could die here — and no one would know except these two.

Please make me a monster. Now, now, now, now. Venomed, fanged, many-limbed.

I paused and analyzed his sentence: Which word had he emphasized, of the four? The second-to-last, I decided. "I have kin there," I said. "My uncle Dex. My dad's brother."

He frowned. I had thought *man*, but he might not have even been my age. And I, at twenty, was what they still called a boy back home. But he was quite a bit taller than me, which had given me the false impression of adulthood. Tanned brown skin, shiny black hair, dark eyes. Aside from the spear he wore little else, in deference to the heat: baggy shorts and a vest made of what looked like undyed deerhide, and leather-and-wood sandals. Stuff only the hunters wore back home.

"If that's so," he said slowly, "tell me his last name."

"Mandrusiak. And his brother's name was Vic. He died five years ago — they both died. My mother and father. Uncle Dex came for the memorial." The words tasted strange in my mouth. Only five years? It felt like much less and much more, or as if the periods of grief and anger, of confusion and yearning, had run on their own timelines while the rest of my life proceeded along the normal one. *Uncle Dex came for the memorial*: two shrouded forms and both of us dry-eyed, last of the line, not looking at one another.

Not for the first time did it occur to me that I had come here not even knowing whether Uncle Dex was still alive. Or still here. Or still thought of me as family. I had not written to tell him of my coming.

"My name's Henryk," I said.

His expression seemed to suggest the weariness of dealing with another travelling grifter, it said anyone could say anything, obviously; perhaps I had ambushed the real Henryk on the road, tortured or tricked him for information, taken his place. I, the impostor, came with ill intent. He'd been fooled before and it had ended in disaster. Never again would he be so trusting. Et cetera.

"You're alone?" he said.

"I swear." Look, I wanted to say. My parents are dead, my best friend is long gone and I never expect to see her again. After what I did this spring the people of my home have not turned their backs on me, but they have turned their sides to me and I can no longer see their faces. I am the *definition* of alone. Plus, your dog would have kept barking if I wasn't, and you know it.

"You had a map to get this far," he said. "Give it."

No point in denying it. I handed it over; he studied it for a long time, his mouth working. I waited for his hand to flash over his shoulder, for the spear to strike me — where? My chest, my throat? Maybe he would use it as a sword. The edge was chipped sharp enough. I was still staring at the spear-point when he snapped his fingers peremptorily in front of my eyes, making me refocus.

"You still wouldn't have found it," he said, wadding the map into the pocket of his shorts. "Anyway, come on. They'll know if you're bullshitting or what. Walk *exactly* where I walk."

A month ago I left campus, slinking out at the crack of dawn — a fresh and cloudless morning promising an inferno of a day. The watchers at the palisades, of which we have few these days, did not challenge me. They're on the lookout for people invading, not escaping. Escape is not something we do. It's drilled into us from birth: *Stay together, stay safe. Stay in the city, stay with your people, safety in numbers, no safety alone.*

Almost I could not believe I had dared to violate every rule I had been brought up with, but at the same time, my fear of staying had finally, and not by much, overcome my fear of leaving. I had no words for what I felt as I passed under the gate for the last time. Nothing describes that level of pain. It was as if I were trying to walk my bones out of my flesh.

At first I moved clumsily with my pack — like an ant trying to manage a twig in its mandibles, constantly overbalancing, stumbling, teetering. I felt like I had to teach myself how to walk again. I had packed everything a city boy imagined would be needed to live on the road, and then some. I made a lot of stupid, heavy choices. Every day I discarded something, and as the load lightened I found myself straightening up to look around properly. And I saw exactly what everyone told me I would see: the remnants of a war zone. And I thought . . .

. . . Listen, you would think over the years my best friend and I would have begun to more closely resemble each other, but I'm nothing like Reid. She lives in an everpresent *now*, as if she carries a bubble of time around her that extends a few inches in every direction. Her gaze has always been forward, with only the most infrequent glances back over her shoulder: not to check for danger, because she believes there can be none from the past, but to refill her deep and righteous well of anger. Anger at how we live, at the world we were born into, anger burning clear and bright like a beeswax candle, not the spluttering mess of tallow.

Whereas I'm the type who takes a step, and pauses, evaluating, processing, chewing it over, revolving in place — a living joke about people who can't walk and think at the same time — and then I reorient and take another step. So I'm often looking back. And I'm often thinking about it.

And yet it was *still* a shock to discover that my thinking had kind of reified itself into the landscape only a few hours outside of city limits: bombed by the past, obliterated by it and the rubble razed over, everything shattered, processed, and squeezed dry by the last generation who could do so. And the one after that was barely capable of drawing a picture of the war-machine unless they did so with ochre and charcoal on the walls of a cave.

I had stood unmoving for half an hour at the rise of the first meaningful hill, staring at the dried-out land, my mind scoured of every piece of language I knew. When I returned to myself I felt that something small but important had broken inside my head — like a chip of metal off a valve.

As I had walked, I had told myself so often that Sprucedown must be different — not all dust and ruins — it had become more than a mantra, something like a prayer, whispered through cracked lips to the scavenging birds that followed me as I wove my way north. And as things became greener, softer, damper, my prayers only became more fervent.

I would leave that behind, that . . . *that.* The world my community had tried to protect us from.

"Keep up," the boy snarled.

"I *am.*"

The dog, head practically hip-level to its master, paced him precisely, taking mincing little steps instead of its naturally long stride to do so. I walked behind them, following the spear like a lighthouse. He was right that I wouldn't have found the place on my own, I realized uneasily. Uncle Dex's hand-drawn map stopped far short of where we were headed now, and I had already lost track of the twists and turns we'd taken since leaving the highway.

The town — was it a town? I couldn't tell — was virtually invisible, nestled at the bottom of a bowl whose sideslopes were so gradual that only for a split second, as we approached, could I perceive the dimensions. But it would have been shockingly visible from a bird's-eye view, with its darkness and its greenness, thinning out in delicate concentric rings around its hidden heart like a drop of ink just fallen into still water. Trees of all kinds, and shrubs and grass and berry bushes with shining leaves stripped clean, and all the strange colours of peat and rush, bog and fen. It didn't seem possible.

The boy turned off the final gravel road and led us down a near-invisible path between two huge blowsy wild-rose bushes. The low bush soon became fringed with saplings and then real trees, twisted black spruce whose tops met and tangled overhead, the shade singing on my skin like cool water. Around and around we trudged, the path thinning and branching, until we spiraled our way into the town.

There were a few dozen buildings, all single storey and apparently all wood — and even after my long walk, during which I'd seen thousands of trees (mainly dead or saplings or both) this seemed stunningly extravagant. Imagine having so much wood you could *build* with it . . . but they did, and that alone convinced me that this was some kind of promised land.

People wove around one another with wheelbarrows and sacks, tools and baskets, paying us not the slightest attention. I thought of an anthill, the way we think of an anthill as one organism industrious and single-minded, composed of individuals who need no description as individuals because their only qualities were being industrious and single-minded. Even kids — I spotted one little girl, perhaps four or five, struggling proudly with a small wooden wagon brimming with round stones.

The boy gestured me towards one of the buildings, unstrapped his spear from his back, then followed me in.

It was much cooler inside, a cross-breeze moving smartly through the propped-open doors. The smell of woodsmoke was so thick it seemed to overlay everything like a yellow varnish, subtly shifting the shapes and details of table, chairs, shelves, two dogs, a mildly surprised-looking middle-aged man who was not my uncle Dex. His curly white hair framed a perfectly circular bald spot scribbled over with the blue and green marks of Cad, like a child's drawing.

"Watch him," the boy said. "I'm gonna get Beau." He vanished.

The man stared at me for a minute, then said, "Well, I suppose you'd better sit down."

I sat where he gestured. "I'm Henryk."

"Mm," he said, and proceeded to ignore me for the rest of the wait. Any move I made towards my backpack was met with meaningful noises from one or both dogs, who had stationed themselves across either doorway, so after a few of these attempts I simply sat there and watched the angles of the shadows change outside. I did not want my fear transmitted to them. A fearful dog was one that might attack, not retreat.

It was strange that they had so many dogs here. Back home, *nobody* had a dog. People tended to avoid anything that even resembled one; the wild dogs in the river valley weren't some native species but pets that had long ago gone feral. They had banded into huge vicious packs that attacked anything that moved, and turned on their own in bad years. The Red Flags were forever trying to steal visibly unaffected pups to start up their own "clean" breeding operation, but dogs seemed unusually susceptible to carrying and dying of *Cadastrulamyces*. Every time it seemed like it worked, a few months would pass before the truth came out — and they immediately put the dog down before it could suffer.

My own feelings about dogs aside, I never faulted them for trying. Humanity wouldn't have gotten where it was without dogs, so surely dogs could only help us in the great rebuilding.

It was a logical desire. Lots of people had cats, which seemed to have a larger naturally Cad-immune subpopulation, but there wasn't much you could do with a cat except let it keep vermin levels down.

Seated near the wall, I stayed as still as I could and tried to study the space I was in without moving my head. Back home, I feel like you wouldn't have known much about me from my own place: definitely someone who lived alone, someone who read a lot, someone who had put a lot of time and anxiety into trying to get backups of things like blankets and lanterns, not someone who said "Oh well" when something broke.

Here, the chaos struck me as a sign of personal covetousness, or maybe I was just being petty and he was the person who held things in common use for the whole town . . . It seemed impossible that one person could have so many things just for himself. A dozen shelves packed not with books but with what looked like carved wooden toys, small paintings propped between them, an enormous copper mould in the shape of a fish hanging above the fireplace, square baskets overflowing with herbs, twigs, small but wickedly sharp-looking arrowheads, wooden pegs from ceiling to floor with things dangling from them: ladles, tongs, knives, axes, brooms, dried gourds, dog collars, iron pans.

"Don't get any ideas," the white-haired man murmured, as if I had spoken aloud.

Before I could defend myself, the boy returned, banging his fist on the door jamb near enough to my head that I jumped and nearly overturned my chair.

"Get up. No — leave the bag."

"There's nothing valuable in it," I said.

"I didn't ask you. Move."

I took that to mean, We'll take what we consider valuable, if we want to take it, and I couldn't argue with that, nor did it seem the best way of making a good first impression, so I just followed him back out. I had the sensation, fleeting but intense, of being leashed — maybe it was just seeing dogs that made me think of it — but leashed, collared, a feeling of the entire community, even people who had not met me yet, telling me exactly what my role was here. A strange animal in their midst, unquantified, unsummoned, and unwanted.

Beau was a big man, tall and wide and flat so that your first instinct was to stand him in a doorway to see if he filled it corner-to-corner. The threads of his Cad infection were just visible at the neck of his shirt so that they would have appeared to be nothing more than chest hairs unless you were watching them for movement. It had come into the whites of his eyes too, encircling each iris with eerily identical scrawls. His thin, long-sleeved shirt was blue, stitched all over with threads of darker blue in fern fronds, or maybe roots, or maybe something else, as if the shirt too were infected. I had never seen anyone embroider their clothes to look like the disease and I wondered if it was on purpose.

A dozen other folks were trickling into the one-room building we had just entered, which was large and undecorated, filled mostly with seating. I assumed it was their equivalent of our city hall, one of those bland multi-purpose buildings where you went for minor administrative things as well as ceremonies or speeches. With one big difference: the benches were all high-backed and set up so that whether you sat or stood you had to face the same way, looking at the same thing: Beau's chair, raised on a stone platform with a couple of steps on either side of it at one end of the room. Inevitably I thought of an illustrated throne room in a book of fairytales. Here, this chair said, is the king.

I stood where I was told, realizing that my knees were shaking minutely — heat, dehydration, anxiety, but it would look like simple cowardice when they eventually spilled me to the floor. I clasped my hands and twisted my fingers hard, one after another, willing the pain to sharpen my mind or at least distract me from my thirst.

"You alone?" Beau said, cutting off the murmur from the spectators.

"Yessir."

"Yes *sir*." He chuckled. His voice was loud enough but oddly thin, as if the lungs of a child were struggling to power the vocal cords of an adult. "Let me be clear, son. I run Sprucedown. And here's the way it's run: Anything I say goes. If I tell Dane here to take you outside and cut your throat, that's a done deal. If I tell him to get a few of the boys and set you down on a chair and make you tell us where the rest of your raiders is hidden, he'll do it. I hope you understand me."

"I . . . what? Raiders? I'm not —"

"Well, I understand you don't call yourselves that," he said generously, uncrossing his legs and leaning forward. "Sounds perhaps a little insulting and Lord knows I myself do not enjoy an insult. But whatever your outfit is called, allow me to assure you, we always deal with you the same way we deal with your scouts 'n' spies. No difference whatsoever. So let me ask again. Did you come here *alone*?"

"Yes!"

He leaned back in his chair again, face darkening. I felt strangely conscious of Dane, the boy finally named behind me — or not him so much as the dog and the spear, his weapons, the physical manifestations of his obedience. There was only so sharp an edge you could put on even the finest-grained stone. I would feel it when he drove it into me. I would feel things I had never felt before. And I wouldn't die quickly: there would be lots of time to regret coming here.

"Henry!"

I spun, stomach churning, trying to speak and failing as the words tangled in my mouth.

Uncle Dex came down the aisle between the benches, one hand out, not for me, I realized, but for Beau, saying it too. "Beau," he said. "Beau. I'm sorry about the misunderstanding. I didn't know he was coming. He didn't tell me."

Beau's broad face barely shifted. "You drew him a map."

"I gave it to him years ago — at the funeral, my brother and his wife's funeral. I thought Henry might come back with me. Or right after, so he'd use it to catch up to me on my way back. I didn't know he would wait till now."

"And why'd he wait till now," Beau said slowly, "is a good question. Don't you think?"

"He didn't mean any trouble by coming. I know he didn't. He hasn't got it in him. Beau —"

"He's family? Blood? You recognize and claim him?"

"Yes, yes." Uncle Dex closed a hand around my shoulder, squeezing so hard I winced. We were almost eye-to-eye now; I had grown and he, I thought, had shrunk, but only a little. The same drawn face, harder now, more lined; the same short, black-and-grey striped beard, like a badger. Everything about him was familiar and unfamiliar. But still a relief. Still someone standing between me and the spear, the dog, the throne.

Beau said, "And we know the consequences for a false claim. Of any kind."

"I know," Uncle Dex said. "And I'll tell him all that, I'll explain the . . . how things work here. You won't regret this. He won't be a burden."

"Good!" Beau smiled, but it looked thin and mean. "That's what I like to hear."

Back outside, walking between the busy ants of their never-ending building site, it struck me. "It worked," I blurted, more to myself than to Uncle Dex, but he still regarded me curiously.

"What did?"

"Nothing," I said. A lie: for had they not just witnessed my transformation into a new type of monster? A small and ineffectual one that would threaten heroes in no future myths or fireside tales?

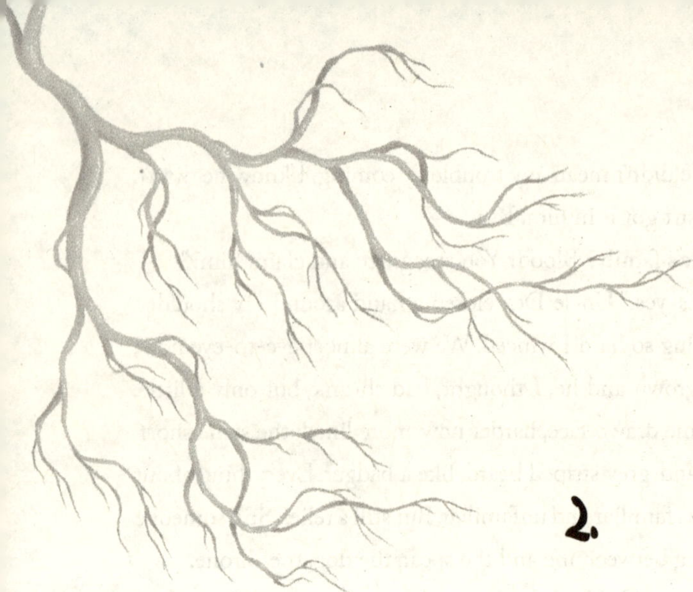

2.

It wasn't that I thought they were going to throw me a parade when I showed up. Everything I know of celebrity is what I have read in books. All of those books (one hundred full percent) were written by people who are dead, writing of a world that also died, even though the authors had no idea that fame (theirs, or their subjects') would be so fleeting and fragile as to be destroyed by a little thing like the end of the world. But I *did* think I was going to have a warmer welcome than this.

Uncle Dex laughed when I said so. "They're like that."

"Was it like this when you came here?"

"Oh, sure." He moved slowly around the room, opening wooden chests, pulling out blankets, mumbling to himself; I stayed outside, leaning on the door jamb, the door propped open with a rock. My body told me it was late, time to think about sleep; outside the sun still sat high above the horizon. Summertime in the north. The heat and light had not reduced one iota all day, a bright dry invisible scouring flame that you could practically hear if you concentrated. "It wasn't Beau back then. He took over about six, seven years after I came. The other fellow died and no one on the council wanted to step up. First thing Beau did was dissolve the council." He shook his head, half-smiling — not in amusement, I thought, but a kind of wondering resignation. Of course he did, the smile said. I found myself similarly unsurprised.

"He's got . . . a lot of rules," Uncle Dex said, rolling the words thoughtfully around his mouth. "It's not so different from your home, I imagine. Human nature to want them, I guess. Feels safer if you have a track to roll along. Anyway, one of the first was *No outsiders*. If you had someone here that could claim you, that was different."

"So if you hadn't been here when I came," I prompted him. When he didn't reply, I added, "He would have . . . what?"

Uncle Dex shrugged, evading my gaze. "Well, at least you and your cousin will get along now . . ."

"Oh! I didn't know you had a kid. Congr—"

"I adopted Dane when he was little." He rummaged in another chest, emitting the hollow noises of wooden dishes. "His mother and I were friends, so when she passed away, it seemed like the next thing to do."

The *right* thing to do, I almost said, and then wondered how on earth he had managed to raise someone as anti-social as the boy who had brought me in, and then decided to keep my mouth shut, since we were family now. Instead, from the door, I took in the single room that constituted Uncle Dex's house.

He had opted to build, or more likely had moved into, a house much like the others I had seen from the outside — not sawn timber but full logs, fitted with square joints into a rectangular box with a sloped roof. Sensibly, the floor was planks, so you could replace individual ones as needed. There were two narrow wood-framed string beds, neatly covered in blankets, and a smaller one in the corner for the dog.

"You didn't mention Dane at the funeral," I said.

"No one asked." He sat on a low stool next to the stone fireplace and used a long-handled tool I didn't recognize to scrape the ashes out of it. "I guess we weren't in much of a social mood."

"I guess not."

Dane blustered into the house almost at the same moment I heard him coming from behind me, so that I moved aside too slowly and the bag he thrust my way — my backpack — struck me in the ribs hard enough to make my ears ring. I leaned on the wall, catching my breath. A few feet away, Dane's dog sat erectly on a sawn-off stump and stared at me with bright yellow eyes. I quickly looked away in case the dog took it as a challenge. After all, I was the interloper in their territory.

"Go get some wood," Dane barked, after calling to his dog — Ada. "Dinner isn't gonna cook itself."

"Oh, uh —" I jerked backwards from Dane's sudden commands, and followed his pointing arm with my eyes to a small roofed structure beside the house, stacked with cut wood. "Sorry."

"I don't know how it works where you're from," Dane said, lowering his voice so Uncle Dex couldn't hear us. "But here, no one's got time to tell you what to do every five minutes, so you can't just stand around waiting for it."

I nodded, too embarrassed to either agree or argue, and loaded myself up with wood as best I could. It felt like wealth, it felt like finding buried treasure — the weight of it, the smell, the knowledge that we were going to *burn* it. And not even to stay warm or thaw water in a deadly blizzard or something like that, but to cook with, and that meant probably half of the heat simply going straight up the stone chimney, wasted. Not like back home, where our stoves and ovens were painstakingly enclosed so that the smoke of the burning trash stayed well away from our food.

Inside, Dex accepted the wood without comment and arranged it neatly in the now-cleaned hearth. As he and Dane made dinner, I parked myself outside the open door again and watched them move — a practised and unspeaking dance, accustomed to the dimensions of the house and its contents, the size of the pot and the length of the spoons. I thought about what Dane had said and whether I should ask to help, but all I could possibly do, I realized, was interrupt this graceful ballet, get in the way. It would be more useful of me to remain invisible till they were done.

There was a plate and a spoon for me, but no chair; Dex dragged over a chest, and I sat, my face burning again. Time to compose a speech about being here, which I really should have done on the road. I'd had enough time, after all. Then again, maybe I would have forgotten it after the minor shock of the mayor threatening me with death and torture. For my first day, I wanted to say, I am honoured and grateful to be your guest . . . no, uh, honoured by your hospitality. But tomorrow you can put me to work. *Should* put me to work . . . I came here to work. I came here to start a new life, find a new home, work at the tree farm . . . you guys still have the tree farm, right?

Christ.

"So what happened back home?" Dex finally said.

"I . . . nothing. Nothing happened." Without meaning to, I reached for my jacket pocket, where I had put my talisman and order of exile, my combined declaration of independence and notification of excommunication. With an effort, I pulled my hand back to the table. "Nothing happened. It probably looks like I murdered a guy or something and had to leave town, but no, I just thought . . . well, that I needed a fresh start. And you're . . ." *Don't say "the only person I thought might take me in." It doesn't always have to be a push. It could be a pull.* "Doing something important here. Rebuilding, restoring the land. I wanted to be a part of that."

"That's good," he said. "We're never gonna say no to extra hands at the farm. But as for the importance . . ."

I waited so long for him to finish the sentence that it was only when he and Dane got up from the table that I realized he wasn't going to.

There wasn't a good spot for me on the floor, so for a minute I wrestled with asking whether I could sleep on top of a couple of the storage boxes, if we pushed them together. But even the thought of asking was too much. I told myself to stop acting like a five-year-old; I told myself I was already an unexpected burden so this wouldn't materially change anything; I told myself I should pretend I was Reid and just do whatever she'd do. In the end I mumbled, "Well, I'll just camp out here tonight," and picked up my backpack and slunk out the door.

Outside, next to the woodshed, I waited for one of them to tell me to knock it off — it wasn't safe to sleep outside — there was a spot for me right by the fire — *something*. Instead, they banked the fire, and the faint glow vanished from the house's small windows, leaving me standing in the deep blue twilight, surrounded by the rustle and hiss of the forest.

For several moments all I could think to do was simply take my bag and my shame and turn around, as quietly as possible, and just start walking home again. But I waited it out, thinking about the sunk cost fallacy, which works even when you know it's in play. When the urge passed, I found a slightly raised spot of ground between the woodshed and the trees, gave it a once-over with a pine branch in case there were any small critters, and spread out my bedroll. Uncle Dex would have given me blankets if I had asked for them; they were in storage, not being used like the ones on their beds.

This is no better than you deserve, I told myself, as I often did, and worked my way carefully between the threadbare layers of my sleeping bag. In my pocket, Reid's letter crackled — the last words she'd ever given to me, the last I knew I'd ever have of her — and I wanted to take it out and read it, but I didn't touch it. It would be no comfort tonight. It would only remind me that despite my airy denials, something *had* happened back home, that I had participated in a pig hunt that ended in the death of a hunter and the incurable injuring of another, and looked at a certain way — looked at from several angles, probably most, definitely Reid's — the disaster had been my fault. Or if not entirely my fault then at least I had been the most visible contributor in the chain of cause and effect.

The worst part — the most painful, unending part — was that I had not even seen the result. I had already been fleeing; I had my back to the carnage that I was about to cause. *You didn't make a mistake*, Emil Dufresne told me, his voice flat and toneless with hatred. *You made a choice.*

I never felt like it was a choice. In my disjointed memories of the day, I didn't remember *choosing* at all; I remembered my head clearing afterwards, unable to remember how I had gotten out of the valley, or even why, what I had seen, what had robbed me of reason and turned me into a fleeing animal. Panic had simply scruffed my body like a cat and carried me away. I did not even have the excuse of the symbiont forcing me to do it.

I said none of this. Emil's twin brother, Rene, had been crushed by a boar, was still in hospital. I thought that if Rene had died, Emil's choice would have been to kill me in turn.

And I felt that certainty, I felt it as real and true as any of my other senses, sight, hearing, touch.

Nothing happened.

Rene didn't die. I went back to work at the store. No one avoided me or spat in my face. I did my shifts in the fields and the kitchens, in the daycare and the trenches. As per my schedule, I pulled weeds, forked compost, and carried buckets. It was probably two weeks before I realized people had stopped talking to me. Even Reid's mother, whom I had considered a friend. Even her. Took a little longer. But she wasn't immune.

All the same, it was survivable; I did not need to convince myself of that. A gangrenous wound: maybe not. But guilt and deserved shunning? Certainly you could survive that. No one had ever *died* of being ostracized. I still ate my meals in the Dining Hall. I lived in my office just as before. No one sent me death threats. I never suffered any strange accidents or incidents. I memorized Reid's letter, mourned her loss, and carried on. A train on a track, chugging slowly but undeviating from my route.

And then Mrs. Cross had died — suddenly and, I hoped, painlessly, from a heart attack or something similar — and the campus convulsed in a surprising display of grief. I thought it was because she was a teacher and would therefore have connected with more people than the average resident — the average name that went up on the death board in the store, mourned by immediate family and few others. This was the passing of a verifiable institution. And I felt . . . I don't know. A tremor. Something terrible and new, the way I imagined it felt when someone discovered that their latent Cad had stopped being latent. An awakening of something unthinkable that had been there all along.

When my parents died, I had been rescued and comforted by the love of my friends, who became my remaining family. By Reid and her mom, by their neighbours, by my own neighbours, by the kids in my classes and the littles in the lower grades that I helped teach and supervise. Because I was a good person, an innocent victim — my parents had been stolen from me, so young, so unexpected. But now, no one was comforting me. No one cared. And why should they? I was the perpetrator.

At Mrs. Cross's funeral, people moved past me and in front of me and very nearly through me as if I were a ghost. I stayed for a few minutes — long enough to see the first flames — and then I went back to my office and began to pack.

I thought about leaving a goodbye note; I even drafted a few on the chalkboard before committing to paper. But they all looked like suicide notes so in the end, I ran a rag over the ghosts of the words, and the next morning I was gone.

And now I was here. Unwelcome in a different way. Invisible in a different way. On the other hand, when you got right down to it, I had nowhere to go but up.

In the night something came to me softly on furred and clawed paws and sniffed me and half-awake half-asleep my dreams became memories became dogs. Teeth yellow and black, chipped from biting on bone, nerves exposed — a dozen mouths, a roiling mass of spotted bodies. Pack dividing, flowing towards me. Desperate with want. I ran, the air thick, fighting me — they gave chase, unencumbered — and someone would save me, someone would kill them, shoot them like a rabbit, Reid would, Reid always saved me — but they overtook me, blocked out the light, an eclipse of teeth.

I woke sweating and stiff, patting myself down frantically for wounds that felt real a second ago. Voices inside the house calmed me more than my own ministrations: people were awake, alive, nearby. The whole way here I had missed human voices. Back home you're never really alone; Reid lived for it, she hungered for those voices, they nourished her. I think I put up with them, at best. But even things you grit your teeth and tolerate can become a part of you, and so they had, without my noticing until I was alone.

In silence, we ate breakfast (oatmeal and blueberries). In silence, again, I marvelled at the profligate use of wood and water. I had told Reid it was better up here — a lightly blustering lie meant to comfort her about my prospects after she left — but it was true. I hadn't seen or heard any running water, but they had a couple of wells, and anywhere you saw more than one well close together suggested that they had a high and reliable water table. And there were simply so many trees, and most of them were alive.

Back home, trees could grow only in the river valley, and we were so careful with them that it felt almost medieval, as if we would be punished by the local monastery whose land we rented and whose woodlands we were allowed to glean — no felling live trees, no harvesting limbs, only picking up fallen branches or twigs, and only so much per person or household, with spot audits and surprise inspections of bags and boxes. The rule had been established decades ago when a critical mass of the mature trees had been cut down or died: Saplings now had one job and that was to make more saplings. Maybe in ten or twenty years we could have a conversation about wood as a resource again. But here they wouldn't need to.

For a few minutes I waited to be told my work for the day — after all, in a place so obviously crawling with industry, they would have a list of things that needed doing. But as Dane and Uncle Dex again began to scrape the bottom of their bowls, I tried to create an opening. "So," I said.

Uncle Dex looked at me.

"What are we up to today?" I said, trying not to emphasize the *we*.

Oh, right, his face said, a little guiltily. You. "A regular day," he said. "I suppose we'd better show you around the farm. The boys'll figure out where to put you."

I nodded, trying not to show my relief. Put me somewhere, please, must have been printed across my face. Obviously I wasn't the only one who could see that I'd used up my last iota of initiative just leaving campus and coming here, and what was an iota, anyway? How small was it? I wondered if they had a library here, so I could chase down my questions as they popped out of their burrows.

Neither of them asked me how I had slept, which was fine. Just because I liked my social niceties (and didn't have to fake it, like Reid) didn't mean everybody had to.

And so, at the tree farm, labelled simply (and in my opinion beautifully: sharp white script carved as well as painted on a black board) *SPRUCEDOWN FARM*, no one said How are you or That must have been some trip or Homesick yet? or anything like that.

Before anyone spoke, Casey and Knox, the two friends I had vaguely remembered Uncle Dex mentioning at my parents' memorial (and whose names I had immediately forgotten, or else I would have used those in my faked letter to add authenticity), shook my hand. A dozen workers arrived just after us and arrayed themselves with the ease of long practice into the rows of tiny trees, some filtering out the other end into what appeared to be a low, broad greenhouse surrounded by signposts of various colours.

"This is Henry," Uncle Dex said. "My brother's boy."

"Hen*ryk*," I said, holding out my hand. Uncle Dex didn't appear to notice the correction.

Knox nodded; he was wiry and lithe, one of those guys you'd hear stories about that began *We never knew he was that strong, but* . . . Under a mop of greying black hair, his face was crisscrossed with scars, some raised into mountain peaks, others carved into valleys, half of his nose simply gone. I thought they were all old, but some still bore the hurt purple of new wounds. "You came a long way then," he said as we shook.

"I wanted to do something new," I said, hoping that eventually the repetition would make it true. "There's nothing for me back there."

"Nothing? No?" He smiled. "Maybe there's nothing here, hm? You walked all this way just for a workout?"

Casey guffawed before I could reply, perhaps seeing my face. "Don't tease," he said. "He's not used to it yet. Come on, kid." He led us between the first rows of trees, a big man placing big feet with extraordinary delicacy in the mulch. The sweet smells of damp bark and growing things rose up with every step.

"Dex probably told you about all this," he said, gesturing at the seedlings on either side of us, some just a few inches high and protected with netting. "We started it, hmm . . ."

"Twenty-one years ago," Knox said. "Not doing it seemed like a waste, you know? You look at the rest of this place — maybe the rest of the world — and we got this blessing and nobody looks at it and says, Hey, this is a blessing. All this water and suchlike."

"So you grow the trees and . . . ?" I said.

"We find good spots, and we try to fix up the drainage — there's only so much you can do by hand, so we put those top of the list — and then we watch it for a season or two. See what comes back on its own. There's a lot of seeds in the top six inches of dirt, you know. All different kinds. Stuff we've never even *seen*, I can tell you that much — plants that haven't grown for a hundred years or more. Then we go in and plant."

"Not only trees." Casey stooped and motioned for me to look as well: a defiantly disorganized frizz of bright green, more like a rosemary sprig than a tree, in a tiny pale pot that looked like birch bark. "Black spruce," he said. "Lot of these. They do good in the low areas where other things drown. Anyway, we make a little going-away package for them — wrap up some compost and some soil and some seeds and some old needles, and we plant that. Not just the tree by itself. Everything grows better when it's growing with its buddies. So bit by bit, it looks the way it used to look. More places for animals and birds to live. And the planting helps keep up the —" He waved his hand vaguely, as if encompassing the whole town, by which I assumed he meant the light layer of living glamour or haze that camouflaged Sprucedown from the casual traveller.

I trailed after them, staring. The greenhouse was a wonder too — not just that they had filled in some broken panes with the windshields of cars, but the sheer variety of the plants growing, flowering, setting seeds of their own on the gridded and numbered tables. A small, round woman moved among these muttering to herself, tilting and eyeing water from a plastic watering can marked with lines and measurements. Far above the squares of plastic cast competing grids of sunlight onto the dripping tables.

"Isabel," said Knox. "Runs the greenhouse. Big boss."

She looked up at us, and said, "B-18. Sorry, don't want to lose my place. Hello! A fresh face. Where did you come in from?"

So I told the story again — walked here, five hundred klicks, took me a month — trying to ignore Dane's theatrical sighs of impatience. In turn, Isabel explained the greenhouse: meant to produce seeds for the "care packages" that accompanied the baby trees, but also to give other plants a fighting start before they entered what was still, after all, a very different world from the one in which they had evolved. "Blueberries, raspberries, saskatoons, crabapples . . . all over here, under the extra ventilation. Have to watch them for all sorts of things. Mildew, bugs, smuts." She blew air through her lower lip, making her silvery bangs flap. "*Promiscuous rust*," she added darkly, like a curse.

"I'm pretty experienced with plants," I said, trying to sound offhand. "Back home it's kind of our specialty. If I — "

"Can you work a shovel?" Dane said.

"Yeah?"

"That's where you start then."

I glanced up at Dex, Casey, and Knox but there was no appeal to be had, and too late I realized Dane was waiting for me to try sucking up to them so he could make one more dig at his useless cousin. I set my jaw and turned away from Isabel. *Start* suggested I could work my way sideways or up and eventually end up here. If I didn't disappoint everybody, that was. "Great," I said. "Let's go."

Work a shovel turned out to be surprisingly technical, to my secret dismay: more fodder for Dane, not that he'd do anything with it, I suspected, except store it all up to launch at me later, with great precision, and for the purposes of public mockery. I was pretty familiar with that. No one dared it when I was with Reid, but we weren't together 24/7, and bullies have an exquisitely tuned sense for those split-second opportunities to separate a weaker animal from the pack.

Our job, at a flagged site about half an hour away, was twofold: one, to create a precisely shaped and sized drainage ditch that intersected the upper water table, following a topographical map Casey had drawn onto a flat, bright red plastic square (used every day, I suspected, from the many ghosts of old maps still visible where they had been wiped off), and two, to segregate the material removed from the ditch by depth. Upper leaf litter, lower leaf litter, upper topsoil, lower topsoil, subsoil.

Dane and I did all the digging while two younger kids, siblings or cousins I thought, named Sage and Ruby, called out measurements and carted away our shovelled material in wheelbarrows.

The day heated quickly, and the young trees around us didn't provide much shade; after an hour, Dane called for a pause and he and the girls squatted on their heels and got their canteens out of their packs. I stared at the bottles, flushed with embarrassment I at least felt I deserved this time. I had left my backpack at the house, wedged into a corner, and that had included my canteen. I just hadn't been thinking.

"Uh," I said.

Dane let me stew in it, seemingly pleased that he'd goaded me into doing the thing I liked least, which was the thing he liked most. He wasn't a complicated guy. For just a second I thought longingly of how Reid would have dealt with him when we were kids.

With great reluctance, he said, "You can go back to the greenhouse to get water, if you think you can find your way there. Dex'll bitch me out if you die of heatstroke on day one. But after that, no more trips back, city boy."

"Thanks," I said. "Oh, and I meant to ask — you said digging was where people *started.* How long have you been at it?"

His eyes flashed dangerously for a second, and then he laughed, a bright, brittle sound. "You want me to change my mind?"

I went.

At least he was as good as his word; when I came back, he gave me time to drink before we started up again, and accepted the extra water I brought back for him and the younger kids, although he didn't thank me and they did.

Interleaved between their called-out numbers and directions, Sage and Ruby kept up a running stream of chatter and gossip — who was going out with who, who was pregnant, who had just miscarried, who was definitely "gettin' senile" but wouldn't admit it — and I kept half an ear out in case I heard anything useful. I envied their easy competence, their quick movements like birds, even the simulated plumage of their silky, brightly saskatoon-dyed hair; I envied their belongingness and friendship. Without Reid I felt not like I'd lost my shadow but a physical part of me, as if I might look whole from one side but if I accidentally turned the wrong way I would let everyone see the cut half, the raw flesh, ends of bones, smooth faces of liver and kidneys where the blade severing us had gone through. I hated to think what Dane would do with that great rawness.

In the distance, a whistle sounded — three short, oddly low-pitched blasts, like the rattling call of a raven. Dane stopped and impatiently motioned for me to hold still; Sage and Ruby had already frozen in place, pens hovering over their clipboards. For a full minute we were a tableau, red and sweating, tools down, ears straining. Then the whistle went again — one long blast. Dane relaxed and glanced at me. "Alarm system," he said shortly.

"Okay," I said. "What's the code? Was that second one the all-clear?"

He sighed, but I had a hunch that he'd answer questions if they were specific and not too stupid — something an outsider might legitimately ask, rather than something you'd reasonably be expected to know. It would be a way for him to show off his knowledge, because some people saw it as a sharing and some people saw it as an elevating — a way to make the other person feel small and grateful for the effort. I didn't care; the result for me was the same, and he was way off-base if he thought he could make me feel any smaller than I already did.

"One long for all-clear or false alarm," he said. "Three short means potential threat spotted that isn't a fire. Two long is fire: head to the wells and await further instructions. Six short is everybody drops everything and gets ready for a fight."

"What? How often does *that* happen? Fighting who?"

He rolled his eyes. "We do drills," he said. "You'll see, I guess, if you stick around. There's one in a couple weeks. On the first."

"I plan to stick around," I said patiently. "You guys thought I was a raider when I came. We don't have those back home any more. How does it work here?"

That stopped him short and he even ceased his shovelling to stare at me, eyes narrowed as he tried to see if I was mocking him. Just above us, the girls tittered uncertainly, as if I had said something almost but not quite funny. "You don't *have* them?" he repeated. "Also, get back to work."

"I assume you mean raiders, not drills. And no, we don't." I adjusted my grip; I had calluses in most of the right places, which I think had surprised Dane and even Uncle Dex, but most wasn't all and the wrong spots were taking a beating today. I didn't think there would be blood soon but if there was, I hoped Dane wouldn't see it.

I said, "People say we used to get them — early on, when things were still unsettled, so I guess fifty or sixty years ago. After most people had pulled back to the campus and the palisades and gates were up and, you know, active. But it sounds like it's more a . . . numbers thing. People who wanted to take over the campus never got enough bodies together, so the Flags would just pick them off for a while until they gave up and went back to the wilds. Then later I heard that the Flags would just kill the leaders and anyone they considered a troublemaker, and invite the others to come live on campus.

So that fixed that. Within a couple of years it was just . . . refugees, not raiders."

"The Flags are like . . . guards? Fighters?"

"They're, uh . . ." I shifted my stance to chop through a root, carefully avoiding my toes in their light plastic sneakers. "The Red Flags are kinda everything that needs doing. There used to be a more complicated system back in the day — juries, trials, judges, sentences, um, restorative justice, that kind of thing. Now it's just them. But they don't have anything to do most of the time." I paused, thinking. "People are tired. And it's not like we have much to fight over."

He snorted. "Maybe where *you're* from. Up here? We used to get these aggro shitheads constantly. I guess someone tried to welcome them in, once, and it all went to shit just like you'd predict. Half the town got killed, and they snatched like a hundred women, even little girls, when they left. They don't want to *live with* normal people. They want to *live off of us*, like vampires or whatever. Anyway, official policy now is zero tolerance."

Beau's policy? I almost said. "So you —"

"Zero." He stopped again and darted his chin back in the direction of the town. "Everybody in Sprucedown's killed a couple of raiders, probably," he mused. "Yeah, I'd say . . . probably everybody, by this point."

"Even Isabel?" I said before I could stop myself.

He laughed. "Her? The older you are, the *more* you've killed."

"Oh."

"Last big one was about ten years ago, but they're still out there," he concluded with a flourish, taking up his shovel again. "And we're still ready to kill 'em. So, you know, if you came here expecting other people to fight for you —"

"I didn't."

"Sure," he muttered. "I bet."

3.

A thick grunt, a statement on its own or the beginning of a sentence: *Uh.* Or *huh* or maybe *you.* Not the word itself but its proximity to my ear yanking me out of sleep in a single motion, pulling my mind up from the horizontal. But my body couldn't get up. Something held me down, snuffling, or chuckling, and then as I struggled with the weight, *Is this it? The official hazing of this place? A gang-rape behind the woodshed? Is this a dream?* one stunning blow slammed into the side of my head, knocking loose the roar of anger and menace I had intended from the start, though I managed only a weak, befuddled croak.

Above me, lights began to appear, showing me bare feet, something furry and indistinct in the darkness. A dog was barking furiously, the noise receding, the scratchscuffle of nails on the packed ground around the house. I tried to get up again, failed, and lay confused in the shifting light and dark until something touched me again. It held fast as I tried to yank my arm away, and slowly I realized it was Uncle Dex, half-asleep, somehow both horrified and unsurprised.

"What happened?" My mouth wasn't working right; I touched my bottom lip, fresh blood in the lantern light. Then the pain crashed in, like it had been waiting for me to see the blood. "Jesus Christ. The *dog*? Why the fuck —"

"Fucking bear." Dane returned, panting, carrying a smaller lantern. "Just saw — dog scared 'm off."

"Oh, as *if* it was a bear," I snapped. "Your dog literally just tried to rip me apart in my sleep and you think I'd believe you —"

"You better shut your mouth about my dog, or I'll call her back and —"

"Gentlemen," Uncle Dex said. "Gentlemen. Please. Dane, you'd better get some clothes on and go get her."

"Fine."

I made it all the way inside the house before I started shaking, and Uncle Dex smoothly moved a chair underneath me as I collapsed. "It's not so bad," he said. "No, I promise. You'll see in a minute."

I couldn't nod. My vision filled with spiraling black dots, huge and orderly, soon spangled with the extra candles Uncle Dex arranged on the table. The left side of my face burned dully, as if it were recovering from frostbite; my left eye had begun to puff shut, slowly but irrevocably, tears flowing down my cheek, stinging where they hit my split lip. After he finished, Uncle Dex got out his shaving mirror to show me the damage: an impressively big oval bruise, bright red, the split lip dabbed with ointment, and a short, curved cut running from the edge of my mouth to just below my jawbone, now decorated with neat *X*-shaped stitches.

"Did *you* see a bear?" I said, staring at the bruise.

"I saw something . . . too big for a dog," he said. "And I saw Ada go after it. It probably didn't hit you with intent." He scooped more ointment from the tin; it smelled powerfully of pine needles. "I mean, as prey. It probably stepped on you when it was turning to get away from Ada, and a claw caught on your face."

"That's reassuring," I said. "Not a mean bear. Not a man-eater. Just clumsy."

He chuckled. "Oh, there's man-eaters around. Wolf and bear both, and wild dogs. They don't come into town."

I winced. *People sleeping outside aren't part of town*, was how that sounded. "I shouldn't have accused the dog," I said. "Dane's pretty pissed at me."

"He's a good kid," he said. "He's still learning that the world isn't out to get him. In the meantime, he takes a lot of things as proof that it is."

"He was telling me about . . ." I hesitated, stung again by the memory of *Came here expecting people to fight for you.* "I knew there were bears and things. I saw some while I was coming — saw their scat too, prints sometimes. I heard wolves. But Dane said there were people out there too. Raiders. And the town rule . . ."

"Don't worry about that," Uncle Dex said quietly.

"So he was just trying to scare me? That's pretty immature."

"No, they're out there," he said after several seconds, choosing his words carefully. "If he was trying to scare you, he was just doing my job, I suppose. The policy is . . . well, after that last time, really, zero tolerance. Quite a few people died. We talked about abandoning the town . . . there was a vote. We elected to stay and fight. And we agreed that the expectation would be . . ."

"All right," I said, feeling sick. "I hear you. It's fine. I live by the rules wherever I am. Just want to make that clear."

"Good."

Uncle Dex said it was highly unlikely the bear would be back anytime soon after its scare tonight, probably not for months, and I agreed in principle, but I was still so nervous I practically had to drag myself back outside to get my things.

The night was warm and windy, lit with half a moon, bright enough to show a few of the bear's prints where the claws had dug in, the scattered leaves and needles betraying its circuitous path from the edge of the trees to my bedding. The rest of the town was quiet; no one had woken up. Our little drama stayed a private matter. It wouldn't for long, though, once Dane got the word out.

Back inside, I helped Dex stack two of the storage chests so I could spread a few blankets on the floor and put down my bedroll. I was still dazed and shaky and angry at myself. Supposing the bear had turned the other way? If it was a big one — I'd look in the morning when the light was better — it could have crushed my skull. Imagine coming all the way here and dying of terminal stupidity. "Do you think Beau would let me have some land?" I said suddenly, wanting to ask before Dane came back in.

"What?"

"To build my own house," I said. "Something just big enough to sleep in, more like. So I'm not . . . imposing."

"I don't see why not. We'll talk to him tomorrow," Uncle Dex said, just as Dane opened the door.

"Thanks," I said.

"Talk to who about what?" Dane said.

"Not you," I said, lying down carefully on my right side. "And, uh, I'm sorry I blamed y . . . Ada. Earlier. I wasn't thinking straight."

Dane grunted, but I still felt anger radiating off him like a half-smothered fire. Like any nudge or the slightest breeze would send him flaming back up again. I watched him uneasily as he stripped and went back to bed, murmuring to Ada in the darkness. Her eyes caught the last light of the fire, flickering protectively upwards as Uncle Dex got up and headed to the outhouse, shutting the door behind him.

"Look," I said quietly. "I *said* I was sorry. A few months ago, a friend and I were hunting rabbits, and we kinda got ambushed by some wild dogs in the river valley back home. But I was the one they went after. It was . . . it was pretty messed up."

A long silence. Eventually he said, "What'd you do?"

I sighed. Lying to him would take all the wind out of my apology, and he'd decide on his own version of things no matter what I said. "Truthfully? I curled up in a ball and waited to be ripped apart. My friend was the one who ran in there and fought them off."

He chuckled. "So he got all the balls for the both of you."

"She," I said wearily. "Whatever. I just, you know, I just wanted to say I'm sorry. I'm not great with dogs. That's all."

"She's not one of those wild dogs. I trained her myself. If she's going after someone, it's because I *told* her to." His voice had gone low and dangerous again. I wondered if he was about to get out of bed and start something, but there were no sounds of movement.

"The wild dogs weren't always wild dogs either," I said. "They're like pigeons. They used to be pets, people used to breed them into like — fancy varieties. All different shapes and sizes. They had names and papers and stuff. And then they changed. So —"

"She's *not like that*."

I listened to the blankets rustle as he turned to face the wall: conversation over. It occurred to me that he hadn't accepted my apology; but I had to admit, I felt better for having made it. At least having tried.

4.

Over the next few weeks what became very strange to me was the disparity between how far I thought I had come from writing a suicide note, and how often I wrote whole new ones in my head every day. Every hour, some days.

The difficulty was not in the text but the salutation, which I felt I could not leave off. *Dear everyone* never felt right, because the *dear* felt too loaded. *Everyone:* felt too abrupt. Then there were all the variations of *To whoever finds my body* and then the mental crisis of a body to find . . . At least here, Reid wouldn't be the one to find it, and that was some relief. I also, to my shock, found myself wondering if *she* had ever considered it — or I was shocked that it had never occurred to me before. She had Cad, after all, and I didn't. I was glad I had never asked her.

Suicide itself never felt like more of an option, always a distant and unrealistic suggestion, like someone at the back of a crowd shouting "Do a cartwheel!" at a choir performance. But it was there, and I could hear it, and never more so than when I went out early in the mornings to cut trees before work.

As Uncle Dex had hoped (I kept thinking *hoped* rather than *expected*), Beau had readily given me permission to build my own place. "Space," he had said, "is the one limitless resource we got up here." To comply with the town rules about eyelines, hydrology, and waste management, my "lot" ended up forty yards away from Uncle Dex's home, smack in the bush. There were plenty of cleared areas that I thought would have satisfied all the regulations, but I didn't point it out. I kept my mouth shut, put my name in the register, and promised to be very careful with the timber I cut, lest I incur one of Beau's vaguely stated "consequences."

In the silvery greys and blues of dawn, surrounded by supervisory ravens who occasionally scared me by imitating the town's alarm bells, I grimly staked and measured, cut and dragged. Merely clearing my tiny square to bare ground took weeks, leaving me so exhausted at work that by the end of the day I could scarcely lift my shovel. This earned infrequent but justifiably exasperated abuse from Dane, who to his credit, and for no reason I could discern, picked up the slack for my increasingly slow pace.

"In Sprucedown," Beau had intoned as he pushed the register book towards me, "if you work full-time then you eat like a full-timer, and if you slack off, why then you eat like a slacker. Are we quite clear?"

I quickly figured out the ration system at the town's storehouse, where you couldn't buy things with money or tokens; you showed your timecard, or gave them a note from Beau or someone else at the top (a short list of names, easily memorized, impossible to fake) saying you'd worked extra hours or were being allowed extra rations on credit. Uncle Dex signed cards for me and Dane, but he was scrupulously evenhanded about it, and never, as far as I saw, allowed any fudging or rounding more than fifteen minutes. Compared to back home it seemed terrifyingly bureaucratic and impersonal. But the system worked, more or less, and there seemed to be few people who needed a social safety net, let alone the thick and extensive one we had so painstakingly woven back home. Virtually everyone worked, even if it was just painting curlicued designs on the houses or sitting (or sleeping) in the same room as the one where they taught the kids, on paper as a "teaching assistant."

It all made me think, inevitably but reluctantly, about war, not the fighting per se but what people did afterwards. Because that was where we lived now, that was how we lived. The climate disasters, infrastructure failures, and governmental collapse of Back Then, with Cad emerging as an accelerant that made everything burn much hotter than it would have, I could not help but see all that as a war. The sides were ambiguous to me, hazed by time and loss of knowledge. Industry versus the world, then the world versus industry, and when industry surrendered, then it was the world versus humanity, till we had all been thoroughly, globally pacified and no longer possessed weapons to wage war on the planet.

And what did that leave us with? A war zone where most things had been destroyed, and worse, into which you could not import things to rebuild your old life, because everywhere else had been a war zone too and they had nothing to sell or ship, and nothing for you to buy it with anyway, and no way to ship or receive it. We had, so to speak, bombed ourselves back to the stone age. The physical infrastructure that remained for some of us — like back home, on campus — was not really a help. It was a place to shelter, but it could not be more than that. And it was a constant reminder of wartime, of losing, and that the fight had cost us the ability to rebuild.

Every time you tried to forget, the entire world reminded you. It was like a billboard that followed you around, or like trying to live at the edge of a giant open pit — no matter what lies you told yourself or stories you told the kids, the pit was a reality, constraining and dictating every part of your life. That was what they did to us. That is what the people of the past did: they took away our future and gave us this one. Maybe not on purpose — at this point I don't care if it was or not. For what it's worth, I do think it was on purpose, all of it. And with the idea that they could win the war, subdue the planet, that technology would simply make a leap one day as it so often had — like in the books, going from fixed-wing flight to military airplanes in less than a decade — a leap that would save everybody, change everything.

But they never did. They gambled and they lost. And as Emil would no doubt have told me if I had ever shared this with him, gambling isn't a mistake. It's a choice.

All the same, here in Sprucedown it was much easier to convince yourself that there had been no war, because the reminders were so far away. Isabel told me about it sometimes as I helped her with the pots in the greenhouse, as her arthritis was starting to mess with her grip strength. "I grew up just a little north and east of here," she said. "A collapse? My grandparents didn't even have reliable electricity till 1971 — decades after everybody else. And Sprucedown, you know, that didn't even exist till forty years ago, so we've *never* had it here. Can't miss what you don't know about!"

"I can," I said. "I read."

She laughed. "Well, I hope you're good at forgetting, then."

So back home, we were trying to rebuild our warzone into the place that had existed before the war, whereas here, they were continuing a trajectory that had always been a possibility. Which was incredible, of course, and I was so stupefied by it that I almost wanted to rush back to campus and tell everybody about it, but I just took it in and told myself I would think about it and not let it turn into a piece of grit that would form the centre of a pearl. Here, they weren't reconstructing a lost world from scraps, or trying to recreate a lost glory; they were simply planting trees and creating habitat for animals not just to make their own lives easier but because they knew what the land was capable of if given a little help. Just enough to overcome what other people's wars had done to the climate and the weather and the water.

Most places, Isabel said, just needed a leg up, not a miracle. There was talk from some of the younger and more eager (I took that as her diplomatic way of saying "fanatic" rather than overexcited) guys about starting a mirror project like this — the trees, the greenhouses, the slow and careful revegetation — a couple of days north, where the tar sands projects had been. But that, she concluded, would not be in her lifetime. Because Sprucedown was tiny and tiny was a good place to start, but the tar sands were enormous, and people might get overwhelmed and give up.

And here, quietly, diligently, every morning, aching from the wooden floor, hungry, I came with my measuring tape and my axe and my saw, and my canteen and a pocketknife. I had a pile of cut and trimmed logs. I did not have a house. But before winter came I would, and that kept me going.

The brush rustled, dogwood and wild rose rattling: something low. I leaned my axe against a tree (too small: not coming down today) and waited as Ada's head poked through the leaves, the intense yellow eyes like she had brought her own lanterns with her. I tried not to recoil as she loped towards me and stopped, as always, still uncertain — the tail wagging, see, unsure, not joyful. *You again*, her body language said every time, slightly incredulous. How could I still be here? Why was a stranger still allowed to live in the town, smelling like a stranger, every single day? Why wasn't someone doing something about it? I knew how she felt.

As I expected, Dane emerged through the brush a few minutes later, holding a woven bag over his shoulder, like an out-of-season Santa Claus. "Hey," he said, and as always rather than a neutral greeting it sounded like an invitation to fight. "Dex says you're 'not' working today. What is this horseshit?"

"He said he was going to put someone else on drainage with you."

"He did, he signed up Kyler, but . . ." Dane swung the sack to the ground and dusted his hands on his shirt. "But like, did you hit your head or something? If you don't work, you don't eat."

"I didn't forget," I said. "How the hell am I supposed to forget with you people yelling it at me six times a day?"

"Oh, so your big plan is to mooch off me and —"

"When have I mooched? That first day. And that was it. Even you know that."

"Well then —"

"It's August," I said, exasperated. "There's more food in the bush than there's ever gonna be. You should know that, you live here."

"I don't eat from the bush, idiot. We're human beings, we invented *agriculture*."

We stared at each other; I had the strong but fleeting impression that we had both just lapsed into a language the other person didn't know. *City boy is another way to say we're always on the verge of starving*, I had tried to say, and he in his turn had tried to say, *I know where food comes from and it isn't the same place the trees come from.* Finally I lifted my jacket from where I'd laid it to avoid the sawdust, exposing the full bag of hazelnuts, cloudberries, rosehips, and early dandelion leaves. "That took me like ten minutes, and I did it while I was marking trees," I said. "And you're the ones who planted all this. You told me that on the first day. This *is* your agriculture."

He frowned at the bag, obviously trying to find something to complain about or a rule I had broken: *Those are poisonous, dummy*, or *Did you get permission to pick all this?* At last he said, "Well, whatever. You're still gonna be hungry after eating rabbit food."

"Probably," I said. "What's in the bag?"

"Dex said to give you this," he said, sounding faintly pained. Extracted from the bag, unwrapped from the folds of a second piece of canvas, "this" turned out to be a longer, sturdier handsaw than my current small, blunted one, which Isabel had lent me.

"It's a loan," he added, before I could say anything. "That means you have to give it back."

"I know what words mean. Jesus." I hefted the saw, admiring its teeth. Loan or not, this was a gift far beyond anything I would have dared to ask for. I wondered if Uncle Dex was telling me *Hurry up* or *I want you to get back to work* or both or something else. "Uh, tell him thanks. And thanks for bringing it. I mean, I'll tell him again when I get in tonight."

"Yeah. I'm going to work."

"Have some nuts," I said, surprising myself. "There's lots."

He wrinkled his nose, and I waited for him to brush me off and then mock the offer, but he stooped and picked through the bag till he had a brimming handful, which he stuffed into his jacket pocket. "Do you, uh . . . you gonna lift that on your own?" he said suddenly. For a few seconds I had that sense of speaking at cross-purposes again, then put two and two together: the half-completed wall of logs lying on the ground at the back of my clearing.

"I was gonna do some kind of pulley and rope thing," I said, as if it was something I had been thinking about for days rather than five seconds ago. "It's okay, really. I don't want you to be late."

"I *won't* be if we're *quick*. And if you don't drop your side."

I blinked at him for a moment, then shrugged. The wall was heavy and unwieldy, the joints between the logs creaking alarmingly as we heaved it up from the ground, but they held. Panting, I took most of the weight for a second, legs wobbling, as Dane shoved at his side until the wall pivoted and we could lean it upright against the saplings at the back of the clearing.

"There," he said, dusting his hands. "Now it's out of the way."

"Thanks."

"Yeah. You better get your ass back to work, is all I'm saying," he said, already turning. "People are gonna notice that you're slacking off, and that's gonna get back to Beau."

"Right."

Ada spun and followed him through the brush, seemingly grateful to be away from my presence.

5.

The canoe was not rocking much — a few inches on either side — but it did not matter one whit what my eyes told me. My entire body from my inner ear to the soles of my feet informed me we were in a boat-wrecking, harbour-scouring, lighthouse-destroying gale, and if I had a creator I'd better make peace with them in the next few minutes.

Behind me, Dane said, "You're not seriously fucking seasick."

"No," I lied.

"You keep swallowing," he said accusingly. "I can hear it. *Gulping* noises. Like *gagging*."

Isabel said, "He's fine. Aren't you, Henry?"

"Henryk," I said, around a retch. Dane laughed, a mean cawing noise.

I stared glassily at the dark, rush-cluttered water inches from my face, telling myself it was fine, we were moving at a crawl, Isabel wouldn't let me die. My stomach heaved; I waited it out. A red-winged blackbird flickered to a stop a few feet away and called as loudly as possible, as if trying to scare me off. I glared at it.

"There's my first one," Isabel said. "Dane, can you —"

"Henryk's supposed to paddle too."

"No whining," she said. "Whining is for dogs and babies. He'll be fine in a minute."

Dane grumbled, but retrieved his paddle from under my foot and Ada's rear, and gave us a few powerful strokes, taking the canoe to a clump of cattails and rushes where Isabel had tied a bright blue ribbon indicating the location of one of her fish traps.

"Right," she said, turning and nudging me. "All you have to do is pull."

"Won't that tip us over?"

"What?"

"I'll do it," Dane announced. "Move over, deadweight."

"No, no," Isabel said. "Patience."

Not for the first time I wished the bear had, actually, eaten me that night; it would have been a better death than either drowning or dying of embarrassment. I hadn't asked to come today. And if anyone else had invited me, I would have come up with some excuse — some fictitious job across town, some errand Uncle Dex had asked me to do, a secret mission. But there were only so many periods during the year that you could get a useful amount of food from the fish traps, and Isabel made the best ones, and it was understood — it was a given — that if she asked you to come with her, you simply went, no arguing.

Kyler was supposed to have gone, but he had hurt himself somehow in the trench — even Dane wasn't sure how it had happened, but he was pretty sure, he said, that knees weren't supposed to look like that. So, logically enough, Dane had volunteered me as a replacement, since it was my fault Kyler had been in the trench in the first place. Isabel would sign my timecard, she said; it was work, after all. And it was unskilled labour. One by one my excuses were worn down until all that remained was the naked fear in my face, and the memory of a pig hunt to which I had invited myself, at which unskilled labour wasn't wanted — and had ended, literally, in a body count.

But I couldn't bring myself to say to this little old woman, who looked like a dried apple in overalls and whose head barely came to my collarbones, that I was too afraid. "It'll be good for you," she said. "And it's important to pass on the knowledge. If you're staying, you'll need to learn how to canoe and swim at some point."

I said, "I wish people would stop saying *if*." But I don't think she heard me.

Heavy with doom and foreboding, I had barely been able to help Dane heft the canoe over our heads as we walked to the tiny boat launch, twenty minutes from town. Isabel went ahead of us, humming for all the world like she was going on holiday, carrying her fish baskets behind her, nested with their lids open. As we had arrived, I had turned back to look at the town and marvelled again at its invisibility: it had vanished into the bush, nothing to give its location away, not even our path down to the river.

Then of course I had almost capsized us while getting in, and in trying to recover my balance had somehow walloped my face on one of the sides ("Gunwales," Isabel corrected me), driving my teeth into the inside of my left cheek. It still hurt; some of the swallowing and gagging Dane had mocked on the way here was me drinking my own blood.

"The water's not that deep," Dane pointed out.

"You can drown in a couple of inches of water," I said stiffly. "It doesn't matter how *deep* it is."

"Stop it, both of you," Isabel said. "Dane, my darling, you are not helping. And Henryk, my sweethead, you are not a little child. And frankly, I am not in the mood to babysit. Now pull on the rope," she said, turning to me, "and if you feel that you are overbalancing, lean the other way. And do that until the trap is up and we can grab it. This is not brain surgery, Henryk."

"Sorry."

Somehow we got it up, the soaked wickerwork stunningly heavy and surprisingly cold, and Dane and I held the wider end while Isabel ungimmicked the narrower one, tugging the inner cone out of the outer and sending a cascade of furious flopping silver into her basket. "Well, that's not bad," she said. "More than I was expecting."

"More than this time last year," Dane said, sounding more pleased than her. He poked me in the back. "Those ones there are walleye, and the ones on the right are perch. You can catch both of those on a line or with a net, and that's how you get the big ones, but it takes a while. Traps, you get more, smaller ones. Anyway, they both taste good."

"My grandmother was the one who taught me how to make the traps," Isabel said. "Lots of people preferred line fishing, including my grandfather — never understood the appeal, myself. I suppose I'll have to teach you how to do both. Next!" She dropped the reassembled trap back into the water; I wiped my face. "Henryk, we'd be done sooner if you could help paddle."

"Oh, sorry," I said again, and wanted to kick myself. Had I apologized so much at home? Maybe I had, and Reid had never pointed it out. Or maybe I hadn't, and I just wasn't having my own incompetence displayed on a fifty-foot billboard every time I moved a muscle. I picked up my paddle from the few inches of water in the bottom of the canoe and made sure to keep a deathgrip on it as I gingerly lowered it into the water.

"They're plastic, they float if you drop them," Dane said.

I grunted to let him know I'd heard him, and then carefully, we paddled back into the centre of the water and headed for the next trap. My heart was still pounding even though I hadn't actually moved much; that was stress, I knew. It wasn't used to this level of performance anxiety. Brave new world, I told it firmly. You're going to have to cope. I don't want to die of a heart attack six months from now because you couldn't figure out that being asked to help an old lady pull on a rope is no cause for a fight or flight response.

"It's weird," I said as we cautiously got up a little more speed, perhaps walking pace. "I know it's a big place, but I was expecting more, well . . . people up here. I mean, when things started to fall apart." At the start of the war, I almost said, before I remembered that I was the only one who called it that in my head.

Isabel didn't speak for a while, so that I thought she hadn't heard me, and I resolved to keep my observations to myself for the next forever. Then she said, "It would have made sense, wouldn't it? We had what the rest of the world was running out of: trees and water. And space. But I think it wasn't that simple," she said. "And you have to keep in mind, by the time I was born, the worst was all over bar shouting anyway."

I nodded, even though she couldn't see me; I was glad I hadn't said any specific years, because it was becoming clear that she was younger than I had guessed, maybe in her fifties instead of eighties. Reid had always told me that if a woman didn't volunteer her age, you should never ask, unless you enjoyed being recreationally stabbed.

"I suppose at first it was denial," Isabel said. "City people always had that . . . protection, that structure around them. Physical, but mental too. It surely would have been hard to accept what was happening. And then it wasn't either a steady decline or one big disaster; it was smaller things breaking and disappearing in between stretches of everything being quite normal and fine. I'm sure people felt that moving would have been an overreaction. Like burning your house down if you found a spider in your bedroom. Why leave everything comfortable and good if you didn't have to?"

I was still asking myself that, but I said, "Mm."

"And after that, I suppose it must have been inertia; even once you've decided you have to go, look at everything they would have had to leave behind to come here. Really quite scary, if you pretend you were them. All the . . . you know, certainly better than my family had. Electric lights, running water, cars, TVs, I don't know," she said. "All that. Hospitals, ambulances. Police. Snowplows. But also their houses, their things, their books and pets and furniture and clothes and . . . well, it's a lot to turn your back on. And you can't bring even a fraction of that with you into the wilderness, of course. It's heavy, having a lot of things. It holds you down. Then I know there were rich folks — are, probably, still — though I suppose they're not rich any more — well, anyway, who built the kind of shelters that they could run to easily, and I'm sure there are some of those scattered around up here. So they didn't have that problem, of leaving their things behind; they had duplicates of their things. They would have had to build their own structure though, that protection, but if you had money that would have been no problem. And I bet they set them up to be invisible, not defensible. They didn't *want* to defend their special new homes from people who wanted to take them. They just wanted to live quietly with their own kind until everything was quiet again. But there wouldn't have been many of those. And you're asking about the great *masses* of people affected by what happened. In the end, anyway, when it was clear that it was move or die — abandon your things or die — it was too late. People were too sick or tired or unprepared to travel on foot, and there was no more fuel for cars and planes. They waited too long and they got stuck. So yes," she finished, "there *should* be people here who came to make a new life. But they missed their chance. And they certainly missed the times when they would have been welcomed in. Everybody's a risk now."

I thought about Dane's throwaway comment about killing raiders, and wondered again how many people Isabel actually had killed, and how she felt about it, and whether I could ask her that, unlike her age, because — at least indirectly — I had killed too, and I had uprooted my life and fled into the wilderness hoping without even admitting it to myself that I would die along the way, and in some way, indirectly again, cosmically perhaps, in the grand scheme of things divine or geological, pay for what I had done.

"*You're* all right, of course," she added a moment later, as if she believed that my silence was that of hurt or insult, being called a risk. "You're family; you're Dexy's blood. Quite different."

I wished she hadn't said that; it only reminded me again that Uncle Dex and I were the last of that blood. For decades there had been so many only children that once the grandparents and parents were gone, entire lines vanished from the Earth. Not that that bothered me, fundamentally. Hubris was supposed to teach you a lesson if you survived it.

When we reached the last trap, it was late in the day and Dane was whining about how long it had taken; if he had come with anyone else, he complained, we would have been done in half the time. I thought that was an exaggeration, and what did he have to complain about anyway? The whole canoe was full of baskets, packed neatly around the dog, the smaller ones nesting on top of one another, and every basket was itself full: perch and walleye shining like spoons, and a couple of furious beautifully decorated pike, snapping their jaws with mindless anger and taking the occasional chunk out of the other fish. Isabel said to watch those ones; even the little ones could nip off the end of a finger.

"Let me do this one," Dane said. "You said he needed to learn, he learned, now let's do this one in two minutes instead of half an hour and go home."

"I'll get it," I said before Isabel could tell me to; and I refrained from adding, *Asshole*, because half an hour was a wild overestimate, and he knew it. It took more like five minutes for each one, because of the reeds and the cattails, and various underwater junk, depending on how deep the traps were and how full they were; it could only take half an hour if we were fishing the abyssal plain.

This one felt heavy — excitingly, stomach-fillingly heavy, not the illusion of weight because it was caught on some underwater branch or reef-knotted to some tangle of roots. I was surprised and proud to realize I could tell the difference now.

And as I turned to inform Isabel of this, the trap caught on something, sudden and hard, and I instinctively — feeling the mistake even as it happened — put my hand out to catch my balance. My fingers closed on nothingness, then on the unexpected cold of the water, then the water itself punched me in the face.

I gasped before I could stop myself and felt the water rush into me, freezing and burning at once, and if I had ever thought drowning was instantaneous, an easy death, now I knew it was not: I had time to think, *Oh God what have I done why did I breathe in why did my body do that why did it do what it did earlier why are bodies like this why am I so stupid*, and to see the sun dim and orange through the silty water, the baskets tumbling out of the capsized canoe around my shoulders, the long shape itself wallowing on the surface, the white of my palms as they thrashed helplessly, then distantly and for what felt like forever the convulsions of my lungs as they tried to cough out the water, only taking more in. Cold burning. Heavy water. The weight outside and in. As if I had turned to stone. Darkness at last. Shining, silver fish.

"It's no one's fault," a voice said near my head.

"The fuck it is," another said. "It's *his* fault. He could have killed all of us!"

"Mistakes happen," said a third. "Don't pretend you haven't made your share, and far worse than that."

A long silence. I opened my eyes: wooden wall lit with ordinary sun, or an ordinary sunset, low and amber. My nose and mouth roared and stung, and my chest hurt all the way around to my shoulder blades, as if a bear had stomped on me.

They had propped me upright against the wall on Uncle Dex's bed, telling one another how unsafe it was to let a drowning victim lay flat, how they'd seen so-and-so or such-and-such do it years ago and *she died two days later, running around like nothing was wrong.* I had heard everything. I wasn't unconscious or asleep, but in a twilight that still felt underwater: able to sense but unable to move, shot through with pain like the lances of light piercing the black surface.

I wished I *had* lost consciousness for longer. By my best guess it had been less than a minute of real darkness. I came to in the canoe, bent over the baskets, hearing Dane and Isabel bark orders to one another, even feeling the drips from their skin and hair hit my back, as they worked to get the water out of my lungs. I heard Isabel whistle for help; I felt every stroke as Dane rushed us back to the launch; I felt Ada's legs heavy across my own, the occasional prick of her claws. I remembered everything. I felt like a bundle of sage, burning. How could cold water feel so dry and hot now?

"He's awake," Dex said, leaning into my field of vision. His voice seemed absolutely expressionless to me: no relief, no excitement, no hope, no censure.

"Let him rest," Isabel said. "I'll watch him."

"Why?" said Dane, now out of sight somewhere in the room.

"We've been over this. You can't leave half-drowned people alone."

They receded, speaking softly about sending me home, how, when, did they dare wait till spring, surely there was still time to travel, would anyone go with him, *should* anyone. Rigid with grief I stared at the wall as the sun went down. In my struggle I had ripped all the stitches on my face and blood was running down my chin again, hitting my shirt with a small *pap!* every minute or so, like a water clock. The moral of the story is that if you wish hard enough for death, death may come for you. Speak of the devil and he shall appear. Call not upon the gods, hope they do not answer your prayers . . .

6.

It was a week before I could work again, but even Beau's adamantine Calvinism wavered in the face of someone who couldn't go more than a few minutes without a bout of wet, booming coughs, so my minimal and grudging invalid rations were signed off on the basis of, more or less, "returned from the dead."

Eventually my body seemed to resign itself to whatever remnants of river still pooled in my lungs, quit trying to expel them, and let me at least walk normally, if not wield the shovel. Uncle Dex asked to have me transferred to the greenhouse, where I gratefully but embarrassedly accepted sit-down shifts picking seeds out of collected litter, identifying them to species level, and putting them in little paper envelopes.

If the bear incident had made me a laughingstock, the canoe incident made me an outcast; it was worse than being back home. No one brought up sending me back within my hearing — I assumed I had my uncle to thank for that, but couldn't think of a way to bring it up so I could thank him to his face. I also hadn't ruled out the fear that the crucial aspect was *in my hearing*; for all I knew, discussions of what to do with me might be ongoing behind my back. I felt as if I were in the water again, this time not sinking (yet) but treading water desperately, both to keep my head above the surface and to show that I *was* swimming, that I wasn't a burden, that I didn't need another rescue. I could not tell if my efforts were working and I no longer trusted anyone enough to ask.

Isabel was pleasant but distant; Dane flat-out refused to talk to me. The others spoke to me as little as possible. More than once I overheard Uncle Dex telling someone, in slightly strained tones, that I would be fine soon and able to do whatever work was asked of me. I tried to see it from their point of view and found myself bitter even as I sympathized. Out of the wilderness comes a skinny but otherwise able-bodied young man, who wonder of wonders isn't infected by Cad — on paper he seems perfect, a windfall of an excellent worker ant. Instead they get this: What a swindle. Not even a useful monster, suitable to bind and blinker and strap to a plow.

The only silver lining, as far as I could tell, was that most of the fish had been recovered because Isabel had tied the basket lids shut. So I could discard my guilt about the near-loss of the fish; I mostly felt, as expected, a deep and burning humiliation at the loss of myself as a person who might be taken seriously.

Wait, no: one more silver lining. Reid's letter had been back at Uncle Dex's place, tucked underneath my blankets. Two linings, then.

I still woke up early to cut wood; everything took ten times as long now, but I refused to give up on my house. People seemed to look away from that as well, though I felt this as more benign than ostracizing. Consider, they seemed to say with their averted gaze, that we too once had nothing; but we moved here and then we built something. So this half-dead, brain-damaged monster should be allowed to at least *attempt* to do the same.

While I sawed and coughed and occasionally stopped to gag from the coughing (Ada often watching for some reason, trailing me into the woods), I thought again about home, and about what hospitality meant there. If someone moved onto campus — either from some other part of the city, which often happened after storms, or from elsewhere — the Housing Section would literally find them an empty place and give them blankets, clothes, lamps, and some canola oil. On the one hand, of course, it kept things organized; you always knew where to find people, it prevented newcomers from wandering around bugging the wrong folks, and so forth. And on the other hand, it had never occurred to me that you would do anything *but* find a place for someone if they showed up hungry and tired and asking for one. Even gophers let other animals live in their burrows.

I had been unbelievably naive to think that everywhere in the world was run like home, I realized, swaying over my stack of logs every night, bleeding from a half-dozen nicks and splinters, wasp-swollen, white-lipped with dehydration. Unbelievably. This was how the world really was. Every day they taught me a new lesson in how the world was.

Along the trail I had slashed, twenty hours of work merely to reach my permitted cutblock, Ada preceded me, a dappled ghost, moving with surprising silence for such a big dog. I dragged today's logs back one by one, and let her supervise while I stacked them with the others. Even exonerated from the bear attack, she still made me nervous; I didn't know any commands to send her home, and I still worried that if I moved unexpectedly or threateningly, she might come after me. And I resented Dane for it too — why wasn't he keeping better tabs on his dog?

I stood in the gathering dusk, hands in the small of my back, driving my thumbs into the ache there that never ended, listening to my lungs gurgle and work. Dane hadn't been wrong when he'd laughed off my house plans. Without help, I'd still be sleeping on my uncle's floor come winter. And no help was coming. I felt again the faint, ineradicable sense of reaching for that last fish trap — overreaching, about to fall. Tilting, tilting. Being pushed out of safety by a giant, invisible hand.

"Henryk?"

I blinked as Isabel emerged through the brush, her silvery hair lilac in the twilight. Ada almost but not quite gambolled around her knees before she remembered that she was some kind of serious guard dog and returned to her post next to the trail, settling down with her head on her paws.

Isabel glanced at the stacked logs, her lips moving for a moment as if calculating, then said, "Do you mind if I borrow my saw back?"

"Oh, God. I'm so sorry I didn't give it back already, I forgot I had it, Uncle Dex lent me one of his — here." I unwrapped the canvas from my meagre pile of tools and gave her back the saw, handle first.

She took it and turned to go, then turned back. "You've got something to notch, right?"

"What?"

She gestured at my log pile. "Something you can cut notches with? In the ends?"

"Yeah, no problem there." For a few minutes we discussed the merits of my tiny hunting hatchet and my serrated hunting knife, and how deep to cut each joint, and the sun hung low as if giving us more time to speak, not setting but filling the small clearing with deep blue light.

"Here," she said as I demonstrated in the air. "Cut one now. I'll hold it for you, it'll be easier."

"No, no. No. Jesus. I don't want to hurt you if I slip up."

"You won't!" She chuckled, and I realized that I hadn't heard her laugh for a long time. Weeks. The thought made me wince.

"Go on and laugh," I said. "I already almost killed you once."

"I can swim," she said gently. "Don't listen to Dane. We weren't the ones in danger."

"Thanks again. For saving me, I mean."

"And you're welcome," she said. "Again."

I lit my bigger lantern, set it on a stump, and dragged a thicker log from the pile, pushing the far end towards Isabel. I still didn't like it; I felt queasy even with her several feet away from where I was working.

"I'm fine," she said, as if I had spoken aloud. "You won't chop my fingers off, Henryk. Worry about your own."

I was plenty worried about my own, but there was no point in stating the obvious, so I let her hold down her end of the log and chipped carefully away at mine, creating the square notch more or less by eye now.

"Stop looking up at me," she said a few minutes in. "The only way you'll hurt me is if you throw the knife at me. Why did you leave your home?" Her voice softened. "Did someone get hurt?"

Yes. Me. "It's a long story," I muttered, shifting the lantern to get more light on the half-finished notch.

"Was it a girl?"

"Nothing like that."

She fell silent as I finished, then she helped me reverse the log and I began notching the other end. "Henryk," she said. "I —"

"Did someone ask you to come talk to me?" I kept my head down, staring fixedly at the bark, the blue-white chalk-lines I had drawn on it. "Uncle Dex? Beau? 'Find out what he's lying about or we'll kick him out,' something like that?"

"I haven't come here as a spy," she said, much more levelly than I think I would have managed. I finally looked up, and set my tools aside on the stump, spreading my hands wide in a

Let's have it gesture, immediately reminded of my first meeting with Dane, walking like this, showing myself unarmed.

"Okay," I said. "So it's the big breakup speech. Sprucedown is dumping me."

"No, Henryk. Secrets are difficult here," she sighed. "I think it must be different where you came from. It's . . . well, it's a fundamental part of getting along here, living together. We don't hide things from one another. It's corrosive."

"What is that, another town rule?"

"It doesn't need to be. We've seen what happens in a town this small, and it can't be predicted in advance — things get out of control, people become irrational, a little like a mob. I'm sure you've seen how hard it is to stop paranoia once it starts, haven't you? Back home?"

I stared at her for a while, trying to place the feeling in my gut that hated this entire conversation, even though her voice was kind, she was trying to be kind. You're being parented again, I thought, that's all. And it's been a while and you don't like it. Because it reminds you of having parents, and of being loved by people whose entire lives were centred on love for you.

And that's never going to happen again.

"I've seen it," I said. "From the outside, I guess you'd say. I didn't really . . . fit in back home."

"You're not really fitting in here, either."

"As people keep reminding me."

"And you're not sure why," she said, holding up a hand to stop me before I replied. "I'm not here to try to pick on you or fix you, Henryk. I'm just thinking out loud. It's not that you've done anything . . . bad or evil. It's not even that you've made a mistake. Everyone makes mistakes, and all mistakes are forgivable. It's just that . . . there's an adjustment to be made here, can you see that? We're not like the people back home."

"I wasn't expecting you to be. Genuinely."

"I know you weren't. But your old home made you into something that . . . well, it's a bit round peg in a square hole here." She knocked on her end of the log. "You're presenting yourself as someone who needs supervision, looking after. A liability. We don't deal well with liabilities."

I swallowed, not wanting to ask my next question. I knew she wouldn't hear it as a non sequitur, which it wasn't. "What do you do with people when their Cad turns?"

"What do you do back home?"

"We . . . give them pain medication and try to —"

"We," she said, "immediately end their suffering."

"Because they don't want to be a burden," I said. "Because what could be worse, right?"

She sighed. "You sound unhappy, Henryk," she said, swinging her leg off the log and dusting herself off as she stood. "Where's my saw — here we are. And maybe you are, maybe you're not. But I advise you to think a little harder about your future here. Things won't get better if you just wait around for them to change on their own."

"Okay," I said, standing as well, reflexively rubbing my back. "Sure. So you're suggesting that I go home. They'll never accept me here. Go back home, where I can at least be not-accepted somewhere familiar."

"It's an option," she said. "You don't have to like it. You might also consider being, well, more active here . . . maybe volunteering for more work, or joining one of the men's organizations."

I nodded reflexively, feeling strangely weary. I'd heard this advice before, and not just once but from teachers and counsellors back home, even from doctors, both before and after my parents died. *He's being bullied*, it would start, and then, *He needs more friends, he needs to be more extroverted, he needs to get more involved with the community, he should do this, join this*. The popular kids didn't want me; the clubs for outcasts were torture. All I ever needed was Reid and Nadiya, and I got picked on for that too. Nothing changed.

"Be careful walking back," I said. "There's bears and things."

She laughed, and I stood and listened to the sound of her footsteps through the brush until I couldn't hear it any more. It was fully dark now, cloudless, stars appearing one by one through the canopy. I wanted to scream, or kick my pile of logs, or set fire to them, or anything to relieve the wound-tight frustration in my chest. Ada looked up, tilting her head.

"I don't have to live in a house," I said to the dog. She watched me, solemn, unmoving. "I just need enough room for a bed and a fire. I could live, basically, in a shed. And then next year . . ."

Reid would have told me to stop panicking about things that might never happen, but she always said that; it left me with the unpalatable prospect of panicking when the thing did happen, and we'd already seen how that ended. Because I didn't panic like she did. When she did it, people cheered at her quick thinking, and when I did it, people died. Someday, I knew, and I felt she knew too, the death would be mine. And she had said goodbye before she could see it happen.

Not for the first time I thought about repeating history — slipping out in silence, finding somewhere new to flee. No one here would miss me. I could be a forest hermit for a while, grubbing a living like an animal, losing my language, finally becoming just another skeleton amongst the millions of unrecovered skeletons from the war. If I was very careful, I could probably find a place to stay where, when I felt myself near the end, I would be likely to fossilize, or become a bog body; that was very tempting. What could be more interesting than being a bog mummy? Then I would be a future discovery instead of a *liability*.

I yelped before I even realized what had touched me, then looked down: Ada had gotten up and nudged me with her nose, hard, in the back of the thigh. I met her eyes, trying to get the message; I only understood her, generally, when she was barking. "I could go back to the house?" I said experimentally.

She turned and disappeared into the darkness, her white tail flashing. I sighed and followed, coughing into my elbow.

"All right, here's the scenario. I know we've done this one before but — " Beau's eyes rested on me for a fraction of a second, just long enough for everyone else to hear the pause in his patter and look at me as well. "Well, it's been a while, and tools stay sharp if they're used. Am I right?"

A buzz of agreement rose from the front row that had clustered around Beau and his lieutenants. Next to me, Dane snickered. "Suckups," he whispered. I nodded; it was nice to know that that was the same everywhere. Teacher's pets, even when they were middle-aged men, took the front. And at least Dane was talking to me again, albeit infrequently and very much as a result of forced proximity. What he always seemed to need was an audience, and if there was no one else around, I would serve. I had to watch my mouth though, in case I said something wrong and he turned on me again.

I looked around the room, seeking threats, allies, knowers of things. When I had asked how to volunteer, Uncle Dex had hemmed and hawed as he explained the constantly randomized rota of drills and participants, intended to keep people on their toes. "You mightn't get picked," he said, but I had, and so had Dane.

The room was packed corner to corner, just the aisle in the centre still open. Sharp faces watching Beau intently, almost all men, a handful of women, Isabel in the middle of a bench, the round silver head half-buried by her taller friends, like a stone peeking out of the surface of the river. Some looking like they were already plotting a strategy for today's drill, which was, Dane said, always *supposed* to be a surprise, but it never was. Someone had to arrange the flags and markers, and someone always talked. Some bored: not paying close attention but not, I suspected, planning to half-ass things either.

Beau ran a tight ship; you did not endear yourself to him by half-assing things. His lieutenants, a combination of friends and less-friendly civil servants, kept a thumb on all the other subtly shifting gangs or factions I was slowly figuring out the members of. It was interesting that not everyone seemed happy, exactly, in their place; I had the sense that, as in families, some of them were there out of expectation and fear, or had been pressured to join rather than doing it voluntarily. I hoped at any rate that they could all work together and that no one would vocally object to working with me, wherever I ended up.

Back home, individual buildings did unannounced fire drills: bells ringing, people shouting "Fire!" and kids holding up the falling-apart bits of red and yellow plastic on sticks to form "flames" preventing access to certain hallways or doors, that kind of thing. It always felt slightly silly. The buildings we lived in were well-nigh fireproof when they were built, and even now, a century later, most were still stubbornly and inherently resistant to flames even without the benefit of their electronic alarms and sprinklers. Things smouldered briefly, then went out. Or the concrete might scorch and spall, emerging essentially unscathed except for a new coat of soot. Here, they had engineered some boggy ground around the town to slow things down, as well as digging a substantial firebreak, a nearly complete circle except for the section leading to the river; but if a fire did start, the dry wooden buildings would go up in seconds.

Beau's lieutenants fanned through the crowd, distributing numbered slips of paper. Another flashback, brief but fierce, like the hot golden pain of a wasp sting: counting off for class when I was twelve or thirteen or whatever age teenage boys are at their worst, and ending up in a group of four girls, all of whom pulled an identical face and one of whom, Lydia Gesner, put up her hand to request to be moved to a different numbered group. All we were doing was making a diorama.

My paper was numbered *12*, which meant nothing to me. I glanced at Dane's: *4*.

"Okay," Beau announced. "Settle down, everybody. God's sake, take this seriously. I only ask it of you a few times a year, do I not? Today's drill is: a missing child."

After this flourish, one of the lieutenants stepped up to the board at the back of the room, theatrically pulling off the light woven rush covering that hid the pinned cards below. I craned my head to look, but he was already reading them out. An eight-year-old girl was present in class before the lunch break, and not afterwards. Her absence was only discovered at the end of the school day, about three hours later.

Someone put up his hand. "Kidnapped or wandered off?" he called out.

"You don't know," Beau said. "Something you'll have to find out. Anyone else?"

"Any signs of animal attack?" someone else said, near the back. "Tracks, scat?"

"Part of the investigation," Beau said. "Come on, Sherman, this isn't your first rodeo. Everybody, go find your teams."

The numbered cards denoted groups assigned to respond to the emergency; mine, twelve, had to compose an attendance list of the remaining children, and then make sure their parents or guardians came and got them. (Eleven had it slightly worse than us, but not by much; they had to play the children.) I wondered how random my card assignment had been; it looked like Marlo had simply been dealing from the top of the deck, but had he really? Had he glanced at me, recognized the Great Failure of Sprucedown, and given me a card to let them keep an eye on me?

"What's yours?" I whispered to Dane.

"Search team," he said. "No dogs though, that's team five. I'm gonna go see if I can switch spots. It'll be more real if I bring Ada."

I waited till he had turned his back, then I followed him to the front of the room, where just two other people were trying to renegotiate their assignments with Beau himself. For a moment I hesitated, letting people flow around me as they headed to their meeting points. It wasn't that I disliked Beau or tried to avoid him — which was impossible anyway, the man was everywhere — but the opposite, which was that I had made so many poor impressions that even asking for a chance to try to improve my standing seemed like it would reduce it somehow. Then again, I thought, pushing forward, heart hammering, maybe he'd appreciate being asked; maybe he'd find it flattering. Who knew how dictators worked when they ran a dictatorship this small.

"Nope," he said without even looking at me, waving off my request like a fly. "They already got enough people."

"But I'm good at it, I have a good sense of direction," I said, trying to sound authoritative rather than desperate. "I got here on my own. You saw the map I had. It had barely anything on it."

"Nope."

"I can help the other team more," I insisted, looking up at Beau's impassive face, the threads of blue and green moving slowly across his cheeks, like weeds in the river. Lizard-like, he seemed to stare at me without blinking. I said, "I'm good in the bush. I hunted back home."

Technically, this wasn't a lie; nontechnically, our "bush" was the river valley, of which we hunted about two hundred yards in either direction of the stairs leading down to it. It was impossible to get lost in. But I didn't think he'd find that useful information. I straightened my shoulders and tried to give the impression that Dane and I were a united front: His request had been granted; why not mine? We were asking for the same thing — to be put where we would have use, not necessarily in the box labelled for us but the box where someone would look for us, the way the store was organized. I'm *being useful*, I meant to say. Not *useless*, which is a dirty word here. Right? And anyway, Dane's spot is empty now, so just to make up the numbers . . .

"Fine," Beau said. "Don't make me regret this, son."

For a while I tried to tell myself that I had gotten lost. It sounded better, less pathetic, than saying *they* lost me immediately. The moment they saw an opening. Because I had let them do it, I had trotted along on my invisible leash, and they had dropped the other end. Six guys that had always been at least polite to me, guys I knew by name thanks to my intense secret campaign to learn everyone in town: Yousuf, Kaston, Jase, Iver, Baaron, and Houston. They must have thrown the prank together as fast as possible, surprised to see me join their team, but it had worked. All they'd had to do was tell me to get out of the canoe and climb up the far bank, "And we'll come back and get you."

It wasn't till they left that I opened my envelope of instructions, with the search grid we were supposed to follow, and realized how far they had taken me, just me, from the site we were supposed to be searching. The river was on the grid, a curve down at the bottom, but not the town, and not the half-dozen tributaries we'd paddled to get here. The guys would be hours away now, laughing at the punchline of a short, unfunny joke: letting the sucker walk back to town. And when I got back, I'd have to laugh too. Nothing worse than someone who was a bad sport about things. Nothing less loved.

I stopped and leaned against a tree, hand on my chest. Fear kept making me take short, shallow breaths, and I had to keep consciously realizing it was happening.

Stay calm, stay calm. Retrace your steps . . . I couldn't even tell if I was following the right stream any more; I had wanted to look so confident, had marched away from them so quickly with my bag and my envelope, head high. And I had left no marks: the dry and spongy surfaces of dead peat, the mats of needles, the moss both dead and alive, it all sprang back, it erased me. Then the dry dirt and the roots, and the smooth soles of my shoes. Nothing here wanted to be perceived, nothing wanted to remind you that it existed.

We had been paddling for a couple of hours, down streams and tributaries away from the main river; so all I needed to do was walk back to the river. I wasn't lost. I just needed to . . . I looked around. No way to climb a tree to get a vantage point, they were all rickety conifers here, growing so densely that they seemed to have sucked the life out of one another to grow at all, and every branch I could reach was too flimsy to take so much as the weight of a squirrel. I didn't even have a knife to cut a blaze in the bark, my God. I had taken almost nothing, expecting to be back in a couple of hours for the big potluck and debrief. I had only the whistle around my neck and the light bag with my canteen and jerky.

Eventually I found a sharp-edged rock, digging and kicking it loose from the ground, and immediately felt better just holding it in my hand, even before I blazed the first mark in a nearby tree: an atavistic sensation, something I guessed some cave-man ancestor had felt in every respect. A good rock; now I have something solid; I can hold onto it; it will do a certain job; I can calm down. Time to navigate my way out of here. Rejoin the tribe. The silence was heavy, oppressive, and utterly complete; not a bird sang, not a bug buzzed. Even my own footsteps were deadened on the uneven ground, on needle, root, or moss.

And then I began seeing my own blazes again.

And I stopped, and sat down under a dead spruce I had been about to mark, and stretched my legs in front of me. I thought: *I am going to collapse.* But I had already collapsed. I could not go any farther down. I was already touching the earth. It was like being so tired you thought "I wish I was lying down in bed" when you were. *But lying down more,* the brain insisted. *More than this.* I stifled a laugh, as if the silence once broken would bring something down upon me. A red squirrel flashed past, leaping from one tree to the next and vanishing up the far side of a trunk. What had I told Beau? Something about my *great sense of direction*, was it?

As far as I could tell, my choices were to sleep rough for one night — the sun was finally going down — and find my way back when I had light again, or to use my own damn whistle and hope someone came for me. I knew the second option was the better one, but I just couldn't bring myself to raise the thing to my lips. If they had to rescue me from a rescue drill, I might as well stay out in the bush, because that was my last hope for a normal life; they'd never let me forget it. The only solution was to come back on my own and put up with the ribbing: initial disaster redeemed, in part, by proof of minimal, minimal competence. *Ha ha, very funny guys.*

The sun was almost completely down before I found a likely-ish campsite — all greys and silvers now, the sun itself gone, the ambers and scarlets gone from the sky. But there was something else in the trees off to my left . . . a reflection of some odd last rays, a refraction on stone or water? A mirage? No, a fire, a small fire. A whiff of woodsmoke.

Without even thinking I headed towards it, making as much noise as I could on the soft ground, even breaking off a branch as I walked and swishing it, slapping it against the trunks. A member of team four, maybe the whole team? I didn't think it was likely, but maybe I wasn't the only one they had decided to prank. Even better would have been one of them getting lost, so that we could share our secret shame, get our story straight before coming back to town . . .

A rising wind whipped the needles off the trees, surrounding me with a hissing susurrus as I stepped into the tiny clearing. I was struck first by how much it resembled something from a fairytale book, or the cover of *The Hobbit* on the wall in the children's library back home: the trees tall and golden in the darkness, the scraped circle of dirt surrounded by fallen needles, a couple of rocks balancing a pot near the tiny fire.

And a startled girl who scrambled to her feet as I approached, her face a rictus of fear and resignation — *I know what comes next*, her face said — who would be, in any proper story, some kind of runaway princess.

We watched each other, both our hands up; I meant to demonstrate that mine were empty, that I meant her no harm. Hers were fists already. She was shorter and thinner than me, very pale, with long ash-blonde hair and feathery eyebrows; her eyes, wide with fear, were so blue I could tell even in the firelight and half-shadow that masked her face. She wore what I thought of as museum clothes, because the only examples that we had back at the university were preserved for people to look at, since after sixty or seventy years of scavenging, all of the pre-made clothes in the city had been used up already. Tight black pants grey with dirt, black boots, a loose yellow T-shirt with a complicated red logo on it that I could not decipher. Her bare arms seemed free from Cad.

"There's food," she said, her voice trembling in time with her raised fists. "You can take it and go, if you just . . . if you don't . . ."

"I'm, uh, not going to . . ." I said, hands still up. "I got lost, I saw your fire. I was kind of panicking, to be honest. I'm sorry I scared you. I can go, if you want. I just . . . I didn't know anyone else was out here."

She studied my face for what felt like a long time, and slowly lowered her hands; her whole body still spoke of fear. Understandably, I thought. A young woman, found alone in the wilderness by a sweaty, heavily breathing man . . . those were the cautionary tales we told kids when explaining why to never go anywhere alone. First principles.

"Um," she said eventually, glancing around. I did too, automatically, seeing nothing. "I . . . I guess you can sit down for a minute then."

I did, cautiously, and well away from her, too far to feel more than a breath of warmth from the fire. Still, the clanging bell of terror in my head had shushed up for now. I wasn't alone, I wasn't the only person in the whole forest, the whole planet; that had been an illusion cooked up by my brain, and everything would be all right in the morning.

"What are you doing out here?" I said, and regretted it at once; her face slammed shut like a door, and she turned her head away. "You don't have to say if you don't want. I'm sorry."

"I . . . no, I guess it's okay." She drew her knees up, turning herself into a kind of protective ball, so that I could see only the blue eyes large and wary over her knees. "I ran away from . . . it's kind of a long story. Let's just say I thought my life would be better being raped, like, occasionally, by anyone I bumped into on the road, as opposed to every single night for the rest of my life by the fucker my dad wanted me to marry."

"Jesus."

"I would have killed him if I could," she added quietly, tightening her grip around her shins till I could see every muscle jumping in her forearms. "But I didn't, I never got a good chance . . . it doesn't matter. I'm never going back. If they find me, I'll . . ."

"Are they looking for you?"

"Probably." Her eyes darted left and right as if simply by speaking about it we had called her pursuers into existence, and I felt a brief, irrational bolt of fear — born of exhaustion, I knew, but it felt real for the split second it existed. Then there was only the muted crackle of the fire, and the bubble of the small pot next to it, and the smell of stewed fish and woodsmoke.

"What are *you* doing out here?" she said at the same time as I said, "Do you want to come back with me in the morning?"

She blinked. "What?"

"I kind of got lost on an emergency drill," I said. "Turned around. Um, the town where I live . . . where I live now, I mean . . . we have these drills, and . . . well, they'll tell you about it at the next one. They don't accept strangers," I admitted, "but I think they'd break the rule in this case. I mean, you're . . . a girl, and you're alone, and . . ."

She shook her head, the fear flitting again across her eyes. "If there's a town around here," she said, "that'd be the *first* place they'd look. I'm better off hiding alone. It's hard to track down one person out here — I mean, you know that," she said, and chuckled.

I had to laugh too, a little sheepishly. "Okay, yeah. But I hugely disagree that you're 'better off' alone. I really think you should take your chances with us — and if they're still after you, and they do come to the town, we can hide you."

"*I* hugely disagree with *that*," she said firmly. "I don't want to bring our trouble to your people. Anyway, I like travelling alone. It's . . ." She gestured at the trees around us, a graceful motion that said something like *It's like this*, this beauty, the smell of the needles, the damp clean air.

I tried a different tack. "We always need people," I said. "Sprucedown has a lot of crops to look after, they're talking about starting a fish farm, there's greenhouses, gardens, there's even a tree farm. Hell, we might be sitting right now in trees that they planted —"

"We're not," she said. "This is natural forest."

"Well, whatever. You'd be welcomed with open arms, is all I mean. And you'd be safe, and protected."

I'd said something wrong again; she unfolded, her face hardening unexpectedly, as if I had brought up some ancient offence. And as she began to speak, I realized that I had: as old as so-called civilization.

"Look," she said. "You seem nice, you've got a nice trustworthy face — and you're a boy. So maybe you've got to twist your head over your shoulder to see things from my point of view. This guy in the wilderness finds me and says he's gotten lost, but he's from this great town, and I should move there. Maybe he's being sincere — maybe he really thinks it would be nice and I would really be safe and protected. *Or*, maybe he's been sent out from the town because they know I'm here and they don't want workers, because it's not that kind of town. They want a young woman. Maybe a young fertile woman, maybe a young fertile woman who doesn't have Cad, or maybe they're not that picky, maybe an orifice is just an orifice as long as it's new. Like, can you please *listen* to yourself? Is this the script they gave you? Was I supposed to not ask, What do you think will happen to me if I just . . . show up there asking for shelter? What do you think the other men of the town will do to me? Do you think I'm not thinking about that? I can't tell if you're an incredibly good actor, or just really naive."

Blood leapt into my face. For what felt like forever, I was so dumbfounded I couldn't even speak. None of that *had* occurred to me — she was right. And although I could have assured her that the town hadn't sent me after her, that didn't mean she'd believe me; she had no reason to. My assurances that no one in town would lay a finger on her meant nothing either. *They want a young woman*: that's not true, I could have said. But it was so many empty syllables.

All the same, the thought of her alone out here — with the animals, with her father's people and maybe her in-laws after her, with the animals, the lack of water, the lack of food — that sat in my stomach like a rock. It just wasn't safe. She could die out here. Very easily, very soon, and alone — it only took a split second of inattention, and there was no help to be had. Except for me. I fingered the whistle on its rawhide cord and said nothing.

She poked at the contents of the pot, then jerked it off the embers and stirred it with a twig. "Do you want some food?"

"No, no. You eat. I have water and . . . in fact, here. Do you want some jerky?"

She accepted a sliver, shaking her head at the rest of my proffered handful, and put that into the pot as well. The wind picked up again, kicking up her fire into a temporary blaze that ate most of the remaining wood, then returning it to the previous dull glow of cherry-red embers. She stared at it with a moment of alarm, as if the brief increase in light were an enormous beacon showing her location to her pursuers.

"You know," she said, "you don't really . . . seem like someone who would try to trick people on purpose."

"That might just mean I'm super good at it," I said.

She smiled. "It might but it doesn't. What did you say the place was called?"

"Sprucedown."

"Okay. How about this: I come back with you and explain the situation. And if I do start getting nervous about your people — maybe they're not all like you, let's say — then I hit the road again. And then we're both happy."

"Then we're both happy," I said, relieved. "Okay. Great. Okay. We'll find our way back first thing in the morning."

"Thank God," she said, unexpectedly. I blinked at her, realizing far too late that she was looking past my shoulder. Talking to someone behind me. "I didn't think I could stall him any longer. Where the hell were you?"

"Getting wood," someone said behind me, a man. I turned, already sick with anticipation, as he brushed past me and dumped an armload of wood onto the girl's half-extinguished fire. Flames leapt into life, the clear yellow light showing the rest of the clearing: scattered bags, shoes, clothes, spears, other things.

The man smiled at me, closing a hand around my upper arm. "Let's go," he said. "It's a long way. We're not waiting till morning."

7.

We approached the town under starlight, like thieves. At the top of the road we paused, and for a moment I was oddly insulted and tried to place the sensation under the overwhelming current of guilt and panic I was feeling — the whole town was dark. Everyone was asleep, everyone had gone to bed. There was no frantic bustle of people organizing an effort to look for me.

The blonde girl at the fire had not introduced herself, but I'd heard one of the others call her Shae. She was the one who had taken me captive, tying my hands herself. As we had travelled, first by their own fleet of canoes and then on foot, she had stayed so close that her knife was constantly tapping me in the back, its razor-sharp tip breaking skin with even the lightest touch.

At least they had removed my gag; I had argued, briefly and not well, for them to consider coming in peace, to join

Sprucedown rather than attack it, I had even told them about the zero-tolerance policy, I had tried every angle of both pleading and logic I could think of to dissuade them. But I had fallen silent even before they had tied the rags around my mouth, forcing my teeth apart, as their messengers had called back and forth to one another in the dark, gathering all the disparate camps, newcomers moving in a quiet inexorable stream like a mudslide. I had never imagined there would be so many of them. They had removed the gag briefly to question me about the town's defenses and layout, the location of the watchtowers, the alarm codes, everything to help plan their invasion strategy. The Undivided Alliance, that was what they called themselves. A nice name. I hadn't even attempted to lie. I was too tired and terrified for anything but transparency, and they knew it.

The leader I had tried to negotiate with, who had introduced himself as Nixon, tugged me to his side, leaning close; his breath carried the burning sweetness of starvation, and there were bald patches in his fawn-brown beard. "One last question," he said, "I know you'd want me to know if there was dogs down there. The wind's on our side for now, but when it turns . . ."

I swallowed, running my tongue along the remnants of thread inside my mouth. "There are dogs," I said.

"And no guns, you said."

"I said I never *saw* any."

He beamed, showing surprisingly white teeth, only his eyeteeth showing the marks of his Cad for now: dark blue, giving the illusion they were missing. "Thank you so much, Henryk," he said, sounding as if he meant it. "That's so helpful."

Do something! Scream! Yell! Fight!

I did nothing. Shae's knife touched my back again, another tiny sting of pain through my shirt, as we walked down the path towards town. I told myself the knife was the reason I did nothing, only watched as the others spread out at Nixon's direction, more even than I had counted at first, as if dozens of people kept spontaneously generating from the others, like a hall of mirrors.

The dogs began to bark, all at once, as if there were hundreds of them, thousands, instead of the dozen or so that I knew of. Somewhere in that chorus was Ada, and Dane must be waking, roaring with anger. Uncle Dex too, getting ready to investigate, not joining his own voice to the noise. Torches flared, lanterns lit, people, my people — could I call them that yet? Everyone streamed out of their houses, looking for the provocation, lights held up like fireflies.

And the Alliance pounced. I wanted to shut my eyes, or tear them out, but I forced myself to watch as the least I could do. Not a good idea. My entire body reacted as if I had struck my head, my ears becoming cottony, my mouth losing its hotness and wetness, my feet losing their sensation of gravity, their connection to the ground. People were falling and not rising, people were screaming, faces appeared for a blink as they stepped into the light, then vanished into the darkness again. It was impossible for a group of a few hundred to outfight even a surprised town of over a thousand but the —

They're not going to outfight the town. Why would they bother?

Moving at a leisurely pace, Shae walked me through the gateway to town, Nixon behind us, his guards on either side. Five friends going for a little midnight stroll. One of the houses next to the road was on fire and I hoped it was empty, but I didn't hope the family had scattered into the trees, because the other raiders were waiting there; I heard the muffled reports of gunshots in the forest, frantic whistles cut off with terrifying abruptness.

Three men had already dragged Beau out into the main road, where he knelt at their feet, a crimson bruise blooming on his cheek already, a big man humbled, naked except for deerskin shorts, and all over his torso I watched in wonder as the disease he carried writhed and twirled under his skin, coursing like dark water under his hair.

Nixon had it too. A coincidence, both leaders? I had wondered how it was that Beau had established this relationship with his Cad — did his work differently than other people's? Different from Reid, from her mother, from everyone I knew? Cad wanted to live and that meant a living host. It made you cautious, made you *want* to avoid danger and risk as if it were your idea. Whether it was doing it on purpose — had evolved to do it or not — that was still what it did. So I had concluded that Beau had overcome his Cad to lead Sprucedown and take all those risks.

But now it made sense. I should have realized how simple it was before. He didn't need to overcome anything and he didn't need to take risks; he delegated. Like Nixon. If you had people who would unquestioningly do whatever your disease didn't want you to do, then it was like you were uninfected. Your Cad rested complacently, secure in its knowledge of safety, while you said things like "Go torture that man," and your people would do it for you, extensions of your body. So it was with both men. Effectively unbothered.

Beau looked up as we approached, his eyes meeting mine and narrowing. I made myself look back at him, trying to explain: *I'm not with them. I'm just standing next to them. Can't you see that I am like you, here under duress?*

You brought them here, his face said.

I should have fought them when they stepped out of the trees, of course. Fought to the death, like everyone else was doing around us; their deaths and my death, it didn't matter.

They would have come anyway, I wanted to say, for that much had become clear as I had listened to the Alliance make their plans. They were new here, true enough. But they came here *looking for you*. They didn't need me to guide them here. The only thing they needed me for was information, and did it even make a difference? We'll never know.

They were bringing children now, women, a few men, young and old, and forcing them to kneel behind Beau. Firelight flickered, making everything seem dreamy and unreal; most of the light came from the still-burning house. Sparks fluttered skyward but nothing else seemed to have caught. Small blessing. I thought of Knox's dreamy face that first day: this place was a blessing, he'd said.

Like their leader, the rest of the Alliance looked as if they had been riding the edge of not merely malnutrition but starvation for a long time. I tried to avoid the thought of who they had eaten on their journey but could not.

But they had not been starving so long they'd reached the serenity at the end of hunger, when death is on the doorstep, when the desperation is gone and all that remains is a kind of fatalistic dreaminess, not "I would do anything for food" but "I wish I had done more." They were far from that. They would still fight and kill to have what we had. And that was why they were taking it from us.

Nixon nodded at Beau: one professional to another, a despot about to replace a despot, on such a small scale that the history books would not even footnote it. "Call your people off," he said.

"No."

"I wasn't asking a question that required an answer," Nixon said. Flakes of burning wood, flashing silver and orange, zigzagged to the ground all around us, hissing out on hair and skin.

"They'll fight you till they can't fight no more," Beau said flatly. "So you better run while you still can. All you'll get from me is that if you clear out and we never see you again, we won't chase after you and kill you all."

"I didn't want to do this," Nixon said. "And you know what? I'm only half-convinced right now that it's gonna have any effect on you, sir, tough old fella as you are. But we're all done wandering. We're not going anywhere now. Call your people off or we're going to start reducing the number of mouths to feed round here."

Beau blinked.

One of the raiders, a big man draped in the multicoloured looped rags of an unravelling sweater, dragged someone up and stood to one side of Nixon — impassive as the kid writhed and snarled in his hands, aiming fruitless kicks backwards at him, nothing connecting. A high-pitched ringing filled my ears: the kid he held was Sage, sister and co-conspirator of Ruby, her short hair in disarray, sleeping clothes drenched with blood.

"Call your people off," Nixon said again. "And tell them no funny stuff, no clever shit. Thanks."

"What do you care?" Beau said, not taking his eyes off the thrashing girl.

"I told you, I didn't want to do this. Every one of your folk that's out there might be killing one of mine; and I'm sure I don't need to tell a gentleman like yourself that we stick together the same as you do. You know that saying about how blood's thicker than water? People always get that wrong. It's *the blood of the covenant is thicker than the water of the womb*. We're sworn to one another, and they're sworn to me. He'll do it," he added, gesturing at the woollen man. "He'll be quick. And do you know why? So we can get started on the others that much quicker."

"They don't care if they die," Beau said. "So I don't care neither. And it's better than living under you."

Because I had been expecting Nixon to continue the argument, as if they were rehearsing a play and I knew the scene was not done, I was still looking at him when they killed Sage.

I turned too late, realizing her snarling had stopped: the curved knife already back where it had been before its journey through her throat, the man wiping the blade on a loop of wool, her body at his feet not sprawled as I had expected but curled, blood pooling around her, bright in the firelight.

Stunned, I sought out Ruby's face in the kneeling hostages, not seeing her. But there were others, oh God, there was Isabel, weeping in silence, erect as a flagpole on her knees, there was Uncle Dex — his gaze on me instead of the girl. On me, standing next to the leader of the Alliance. On the side of the murderers.

Beau muttered something at last, unintelligible, his face ashen; asked to repeat it, he only grunted, and finally he managed to convey something to the guard behind him, who walked over to us and stooped and tugged something away from the dead girl — a wooden whistle, on a loop of rawhide like mine, around her neck.

Then he blew five short blasts, again and again, and we waited, in the smoke and the roar of the house, its thick timbers crumbling to the stone foundation, and the whistle sounded again, so that my teeth shook in their sockets, so the scar on my face seemed about to shake itself apart, and slowly the missing of Sprucedown returned to us, and still no one screamed, or spoke.

"Thank you." Nixon turned to his executioner. "Him next," he said, pointing at Beau. "And then we'll talk about the rest;

I'd like some breakfast, and then we can discuss who'd like to cooperate with us on a go-forward basis."

He glanced at me as if he had forgotten I existed, and his face brightened. "And I'd like to thank you for not interfering," he said. "Very neighbourly of you. Shae, put him with the others. His work's done. I'm going to go eat."

As I followed Shae, I wondered whether there were different kinds of death, different degrees of death. Something under my breastbone felt dead, an uneasy stillness, like going into a room and not seeing your pet's chest rise and fall with its sleeping breath; and since the breastbone shielded many things that I knew were essential to life, surely I had died. So how was I still walking? Still moving?

Sage and all that blood on the street. Right in the middle of the street, where we — or the raiders — where people, anyway, would pass every day. Putting our blasphemous, our dirty feet on her blood.

Shae led me past the storeroom, stopping when someone hailed her from the doorway. I peered over her shoulder at a poorly-lit scene from a medieval woodcut, maybe a warning about the fate of gluttons in hell. The Alliance was falling upon Sprucedown's stores with a kind of terrifying orderliness, savaging the wooden crates and reed sacks, kicking at barrel lids that would not come loose, grunting and snarling and yet somehow not losing a speck of food. A dried berry that seemed to be a spot of shadow was clocked at once and recovered from the wooden floor, held carefully between a bloody thumb and forefinger, much too precious to lose. They ate the same way — ravenous, gulping and nearly choking, without speaking. I had thought Nixon would have to reprimand them for making a mess, because I had expected a mess, but they were like clean animals. Unthinking in their violence but also frantic to polish their plates.

"Just a minute," Nixon said from within, getting up and wiping his mouth on his sleeve. "Lost Boy. You seem relatively bright." He put a hand absently over the new, visible bulge in his stomach, the way people do sometimes when they are pregnant, protecting the roundness full of life. The image sickened me. He went on, "Brighter than a lot of these folks, hmm? If they hadn't overreacted, we'd all be getting along right now. Eating together."

"Mm," I said, trying to keep my voice neutral, not condoning him, not judging, God forbid, not making him angry at me.

"You might make a good liaison between the new folks and the old," he mused. "You know. A trusted go-between."

I laughed despite myself. "They don't trust me," I said. "I'm too new here. I just came at the start of the summer. A few months ago. They don't like . . . new things."

"Well, I can see that." He rubbed his belly again, smiling. "Still. We've put a lot of thought into this plan over the years, and you or someone like you was always going to be part of it, if we could find someone to fill the position. You're on our side now, and I think that's a good place to begin to bring other folks over. Don't you?"

I'm not on your side. I didn't agree to anything. There was a knife in my back; the cuts still itch and burn. I will not be your tool, I will not be the blunt instrument you yourself refuse to wield. Or your disease does, or whoever. *No. No.* I said, "Can I think about it?"

"Please, I insist."

Shae yanked on my arm, and we moved down the street, joining other Alliance people with captives of their own — some with one or two, some with more, roped into a long chain behind them. *Zero tolerance* only worked if you were both fighting to kill; I suspected they had not had too many drills or much training on what to do if you had been disarmed and captured by people who were done fighting you. No one looked at me as we passed under the torches of two guards flanking the open door of the schoolroom. It was already nearly full of people sitting on the floor, slumped between desks and chairs, hands looped with pale twine to each other and to the furniture and even the hooks on the walls. I looked around frantically as Shae shoved me in and shut the door behind me: Uncle Dex? Isabel? Dane? No, or if they were in here, their faces had not been upraised in that last moment of brightness.

I squeezed into a spot against the wall next to the door, someone pressing me on either side, my shoulders aching and wrists burning where they were crushed between my back and the wood. No one spoke. Were there Alliance guards inside as well? Must be. And there were more guards outside than just the ones at the doors — I could see their heads and shoulders pacing in front of the windows, which had been set up high so the younger kids couldn't reach them.

It was still dark outside and part of me simply could not believe that the night was not yet over, that the only light still came from the moon, hazy through a low-lying layer of woodsmoke trapped between the buildings and not blowing away. It always smelled like woodsmoke here, but the breeze coming in through the windows was an assault, and I tried to stifle my coughing but could not. It seemed to require every muscle in my body. As if I had given them permission, other people began to cough as well, a few at first, then more.

"Can we have some water, you bastards?" someone called.

"Fuck off," one of the window guards said.

"Water!" someone else yelled, a woman. "Come on, there's kids in here!"

"Everybody shut up!" One of the guards hammered on the wall from the outside, startlingly near where I was leaning. "Or we'll come in there and shut you up!"

As the room devolved into overlapping voices saying things like *We should just do what we're told* and *I don't care if they kill me* and *At least let us get water for the kids*, something else thumped violently against the wall at my back, and I squirmed away from it. "All right already!" I yelled, losing my temper. It wasn't like anyone would hear me over the commotion, and worse yet, I began to cough again. "You got what you wanted, you don't need to act like pricks now!"

Cold, smoky air rushed in, a fresh draft blasting between the windows and what I belatedly realized was the open door behind me. I backed up again quickly, trying to get a shoulder up in case the guard felt like smacking me around for yelling — but whoever it was only stood in the doorway for a moment, torchless, something gleaming in one hand. "Okay," came a familiar voice. "If you can run, run."

"Hey!" someone said in the far corner of the room. "Who the fuck is that?"

That was Dane, and I hoped he wasn't alone, because as I scrambled to my feet and tripped over people getting to the door, I realized that just a handful of people were following me — people who hadn't been tied up, or hadn't been tied up properly, but also Alliance guards in hot pursuit, hampered just as I was by the dark and the crowd. "They got people in there!" I gasped as I passed Dane in the doorway. "Untie me!"

"Get clear!" he snapped, not turning to look at me. As I stumbled into the main road, dazed, a handful of people moved past me from the trees, flashes of pale faces and hands like scraps of moonlight between the birches: Yousuf, Baaron, Houston, the men who had dumped me in the woods. Their clothes looked black and heavy with blood. They moved swiftly, like the small predators that filled these woods, martens, weasels, wolverines, flowing to Dane's side as the guards burst out of the room. One guard hung back for a moment before joining the fight, having the presence of mind to signal the others with the small, high-pitched metal pipes they carried.

We might have seconds before more Alliance people showed up — they had had to split up the captives into the bigger buildings, so they would be spread out, but the town wasn't big enough for that to pose much of an issue. But if they would come when they were called —

Awkwardly, I sidled to the side of the schoolroom; my heart pounding, waiting at any moment to be ambushed and throttled. But all the fighting seemed to be at the front of the building. Here there were only bodies, ragged and unfamiliar clothing and faces, where Dane and the others must have leapt on them in the darkness. No weapons, but there was still something to salvage from the dead. I grabbed one pipe, snapping it from its string, and debated another. But no: footsteps already approaching, shouting coming our way.

"Come on!" Dane hissed, appearing next to me like a ghost; he stank of fresh blood. "Told everyone to split up. Get to the trees!"

We did not look back to see if the others were following us, but turned our backs on the town and ran.

8.

It felt like a dream, the logic of a dream. Because it seemed so impossible that I had escaped them, the enemy, just as in a dream it feels impossible, and you imagine their pursuit with such dread and such graphic consequence that you call it to you, because in a dream what you fear is given life by the fear, is given form and body and a pulse and a voice. I felt I must be leaving it behind me in a trail, thick as smoke and just as visible. They could follow me by it, as if by a thread I had left behind me.

But no one came, and we worked our way uphill from the town in silence via a complicated route of turns and switchbacks I had never seen before. I was on the verge of collapse when Dane finally held up a hand for a halt, and I found we had stopped in a tiny clearing about three yards across, tightly ringed by tall half-dead pine trees.

For a long time we did not speak; with a start I realized that the sun was coming up, and that I was desperately hungry and tired, and that I hadn't eaten or slept for a full day and that neither of those things mattered. Light filtered grey and clean through the trees, pre-dawn light, fragile and thin as glass. No smoke out here and no smell of it.

Dane's shirt and shorts were soaked in blood, and his bare feet and his shins too, as if he had been wading through it; he still carried his spear, darkened from the tip to halfway down the haft. Unspeaking, he took a knife from his pocket and sawed through the rope around my wrists. I drew my hands painfully upwards to look at them: swollen and purple, as if they had been crushed.

"The others," I said, and stopped to cough again. "Yousuf, Baaron —"

"I told them to split up," he said. "Lose everybody in the woods. The more we're spread out, the more they gotta spread out to find everyone."

"Where's Ada?"

"We got separated," he said. "I don't know. She was next to me, and then I looked down and she was gone. Just after they killed Beau."

"You saw?"

"I was there. In the trees." At last either the shock or the journey caught up to him and he sat down suddenly, almost a controlled fall, catching himself on one outflung hand. I sat too, more clumsily. The clearing was so small that our feet were inches apart.

"The head guy," he went on, his voice shaking. "After the first wave of the attack I knew exactly what they'd do: try to encircle the town. Like a fish trap. To get it back, you need to break the circle from the outside. You can't do it from inside. So I got out of the house as soon as Ada started barking. Grabbed my spear and ran for the woods. Away from the town. Out of containment. Found a few others to help. Not many."

"They were *in* the woods. There were dozens of them."

"Yeah, there were a lot," he agreed, leaning his head against the trunk behind him, eyes closed. "Way more than in town, as it turned out. Me and the guys got every one we could find. The circle will be thin now." He chuckled, a small humourless noise like the rattle of a raven.

I stared at him. With his eyes closed, he seemed far younger than I had ever seen him — like a child, nine or ten years old, dozing off as we told stories by the fire. *Got every one we could find.* How many had he killed? I knew he hadn't been keeping count. Maybe he did not even know — I thought I wouldn't, if it had been me there in the dark, ambushing and stabbing and fleeing, creeping up on people like a mountain lion on silent paws. I wondered if any of the blood on his clothes was his. "Have you done that before?" I said slowly. "Killed people?"

He shook his head, eyes still shut.

So you were *all talk that day*, I wanted to say, but that was pointless. It didn't matter. Words didn't matter now. They hadn't helped us. I said, "I told Dex I came out here because I was bored back home. Wanted a fresh start. I joked that it looked like I killed a guy, but that wasn't it. Well, I did. Not me personally. But someone died."

He opened his eyes at last and focused on me, his face unmoving.

"My best friend got invited on a boar hunt," I said. "I wanted to go too. I don't know why. It was a stupid thing to do. And they didn't want me there, but she talked them into giving me an — an easy job. All I had to do was stand there. Make sure there was a *circle*." I held down a laugh, knowing it would just make me cough again. My chest ached, a deep, wrenching agony of pulled or torn muscle. "I panicked and ran. And worse than that, I did it when everything was moving — when they really needed the circle to be closed. One guy died. Another guy had his back broken."

A long silence. I waited for Dane to show disgust, anger, something. But he only said, flatly, as if uninterested, "Did they get any boars?"

"Why the fuck," I said, trying to keep my voice from shaking, "would that matter? Why would you *ask* that?"

He shrugged. "People die all the time," he said. "Survivors gotta eat."

I dropped my head into my hands, then raised it with a monumental effort. "Anyway," I said. "What I *meant* to say was: Thank you for breaking us out. And if . . . if you'll let me stay with you and fight, then you can trust that I'll stand my ground. Because I've thought about it. And I don't want to run any more."

"You'd be useless in a fight."

"I might be able to help with other stuff," I said. I took the Alliance pipe out of my pocket and tossed it to him; he didn't get a hand up in time, and the little piece of metal landed in his lap. "That's one of their whistles. You probably heard them. They don't sound like ours. I heard a bunch of their signals while I was —" I swallowed before I could say *with them in the woods*. That was a story Dane didn't need to hear right now. "— in the school," I finished.

"Hmm." He picked it up, turning it around in the slowly strengthening light. "So you think you could like . . . fake their calls? Move them around?"

"I think so."

"I took all their shit," Dane added after a minute.

"What?"

"Their bows and arrows and guns and stuff. Everything I could find. Couldn't carry everything in one trip, but it's like . . ." He sucked his teeth, thinking. "Three, four stashes. If we get all that . . ."

"What the hell are two people supposed to do with twenty crossbows?"

"Give them away." He threw the metal pipe back at me.

"How?"

"Get up. I'll figure it out on the way."

The core problem with Sprucedown, it turned out, was that it was *too* defensible; it was like a medieval castle, specifically sited, planned, and built to withstand an attack from the outside. And with its watchtowers and the lack of trails around it, needing to enter via the long spiraling route Dane had used on the first day, it was built to be invisible first — to have invisibility as the first defense, to be like a fawn in the brush, unmoving as a stone and easily passed by. So Dane's plan had been to turn that inside out: How best would you keep Sprucedown your own, if you were a raider who had taken it over?

His theory was that the Alliance would pull their people into the perimeter of the town. If they figured they had captured or killed the majority of the townsfolk, there was no need to patrol the woods any more and a much greater need to contain whoever was left in town. Frankly, Dane said, in a voice so cold it made my hair stand on end, it might be the case that there was no one in Sprucedown left to rescue; if Nixon could so callously order the execution of a teenage girl, he would have no compunction about killing quite literally everyone else.

My argument (which sounded weak even to me) was that Nixon would probably spare some of the Sprucedowners for strictly practical reasons: women to dole out to his predominantly male followers; children to raise as their own; maybe elders who didn't seem too ornery and could still work to produce food.

"He *said* they'd kill anyone who didn't cooperate," Dane snapped. "If he really meant that, then it's everyone, because I don't think any one of us would knuckle under and join them. They wouldn't turn their back on us. Like bears."

"Like bears what?"

"Sometimes if there's a sow and a bear wants her, he'll kill her cubs so she comes back into heat to mate with him.

And sometimes that backfires. She'll try to defend them, or she'll attack him after he kills them. So sometimes he ends up killing all of them. Cubs, mother, all. Just to make sure he's safe."

"Jesus Christ," I said.

We sat half-buried in a kind of hunter's blind of damp moss, excavated with our bare hands just deep enough to let us hide from a casual glance; Dane insisted on it every time we stopped. I studied my bare toes as he talked. I had abandoned my soaked boots hours ago, anticipating this last phase of the journey, which would be wet and surreptitious and fast if we were doing it right.

Around us birds flicked back and forth, not singing, intent on feeding themselves and doing nothing else. Somewhere nearby a raven gurgled to itself, as if trying to get a baby to sleep. I hoped it wouldn't make alarm calls when we started moving again. For the millionth time I thought about leaving — north, east, it didn't matter, becoming the tiny dot in the wilderness that I had genuinely thought Shae was. Living alone, safe and abandoned. Becoming bones out there. White, picked clean, bleached like chalk. I had seen many on my walk here. Because it was just the two of us against the whole band of scavengers, and that wasn't how I wanted to die. I wanted a quieter death.

Dane said, "Can you fucking grow a pair? We'll be okay if you just do like I tell you."

I wanted to tell him how utterly impossible it was for me to do otherwise — that the only thing keeping me semi-functional through my paralyzing fear was that he had a plan, and he had given me clear instructions as to my part in the plan — but I said, "I will."

He looked doubtful. I didn't blame him. "We'll only get one shot at this. If you fuck up —"

"If *either* of us fucks up."

Still we sat there, in the sun diluted by high, hazy clouds, not casting shadows on the wet ground; I was shivering, chilled by the damp earth. We had eaten, but not enough; we had kept watch so we could sleep, but that too had not been enough. I felt like you'd have to put us together to add up to a whole man.

Dane hefted the bundle of weapons we had retrieved: spears, unloaded crossbows, plastic canisters of bolts, one gun and a handful of loose bullets in a greasy denim pouch. His plan, if you could call it that, was simple — create a distraction at one of the watchtowers, slip away, free and arm any remaining captives. After that, the townsfolk would do what they did best. Fight back. To the death.

"Odds are better than yesterday," he'd said, "number-wise."

And I thought again about the Flags back home and the board in the store where I worked, on the back wall so everyone saw it when they came in, deaths updated every morning, and how I had come from a place where I was surrounded by death (but not murder) to this, where we planned it out meticulously, where it was premeditated and calculated, where I was the *only* one unused to the math of my life or their life. The life of my people versus the life of a stranger. In versus out. They had been ready to kill me just a few months ago.

"What if there's no one to save?" I said.

"Then we just kill the outsiders," he said, bobbing his free shoulder as if we were discussing a hen that had stopped laying.

Why? I almost asked. It doesn't bring back the dead. They'll kill you too, before you can enjoy even the faintest taste of revenge; you will throw your life away for nothing.

But I thought I knew what he'd say if I asked. He would tell me that sometimes people forfeited their right to be alive — not just in his opinion, but in some vague and nebulous way in the eyes of the universe, in the spirit of a world that was at least slightly alive and filled with knowing at some level we could not comprehend, in the way of that world, those people no longer deserved life; they had proven it, they had filled out the paperwork with all the evidence to show it, with every one of our people that they killed simply for living in the town that the scavengers wished to overtake — for being a bear cub from the wrong mother. He would be merely the tool of this universal correction or readjustment; he would do it because it must be done. Because they should not be alive any more, that is what he would say. *Should not.*

"You're not gonna fucking chicken out at the last minute, are you?" he said, narrowing his eyes. "Now that you told me about your track record?"

"I'm gonna need you to not bring that up," I said.

He looked as if he were about to say something else, then pressed his lips together and nodded.

The watchtowers were not prominent, and had not been constructed to be; they were more like deer blinds. About half were attached to trees thick enough to bear their weight, and where the trunks were too thin or there were not enough trees, they had been built to mimic a cluster of spruce trees, covered in glued-on bark like a building's brick facade so that the raw wood did not show. But Dane knew where they all were, and in our own light disguise of spruce branches and mud, we crept at a snail's pace towards the tower he had chosen, the last one on the not-quite-closed circle surrounding the town near the river, where it was too wet for anyone to move easily and so they had not bothered putting them up there.

My heart was hammering, less in my chest than in my ears, so that I could barely hear how much noise we were making. Only Dane's motion kept me in motion. *I don't want to*, I thought every time I lifted a foot. *I don't want to. I don't want to.*

A shadow moved in the watchtower, nothing we would have seen unless we were looking for it; I froze behind Dane, and we watched the guard for the body language that would suggest he had seen us and was about to raise the alarm. I wished we had come upon him asleep; I wished he was as tired as we were.

For a long time we crouched there unmoving. Then the guard turned, lazily, ninety degrees, looking west and putting his back cleanly to us. Again we moved in silence, on all fours, and then we were at the base of the tower and out of his field of vision. Dane's eyes bored into mine, already hot and accusatory: *Don't fuck up!*

Don't fuck up. Dane needed speed; I needed luck. I took a deep breath, took out the signal whistle, and blew into it. Three short, two long: the signal for *Come over here! Follow the sound!*

The guard spun, startled, and instead of going for his weapon, stood frozen, scanning the horizon, then went to the edge of the little enclosure and swivelled his head frantically back and forth, looking for wherever the noise was coming from. I kept blowing, my hands shaking, expecting a crossbow bolt through the head any second, Jesus, where was Dane? There: eeling up the ladder at top speed, lizardquick with his muddy hands.

The scuffle was brief; I could see only their shoulders and heads for the few seconds it lasted. All I could think about was Dane in the dark last night, my deadly cousin, just like this, winning fights with people twice his size because he went nuclear right away. There was no preamble, no feinting, no sizing up the opponent, no insults, no fake-outs; it was full violence, full speed, immediately.

I waited until the platform stopped shaking, then climbed up, my arms and legs trembling and my hands sweating so much that they slipped even on the irregular, bark-covered rungs.

There wasn't really room up there for three people; Dane shoved the bloody bundle of the raider off the platform to make room. I didn't bother asking if the man was dead or unconscious. With the cracked monocular chained to the watchtower we took turns looking back at Sprucedown.

My heart hurt at how ordinary it looked — how it did not look like a war zone, only that the paths were empty, the bustle that I was used to between buildings gone now. There was the scar of Mr. Palmer's burnt house, black and grey. There was the roof of my own little house, in its clearing far from the others. I had only last week finished building a chair for it, so I didn't have to sit in my bed all the time. Next I would build a table, if I was still alive. A small one, fitting into the corner.

"There," Dane said quietly. "There's definitely people in the timber shed. A lot of people."

I took the monocular from him and studied the long wooden building. I couldn't see people, but it was clear enough that the Alliance was guarding it: two guards at each door, and a full perimeter around the walls. Guess they learned their lesson from the school.

We clambered back down to ground level, recovering our unwieldy load of weaponry, tied with shoelaces and belts scavenged from the dead. Dane pulled the whistle off the guard, snapping the rawhide, and looked at me: *Ready?*

I nodded. *Ready.* "Remember," I said. "Three short, two long calls people towards you. That's what they use for reinforcements. Two short is *head north*. Three short is east, two long is south, three long is west."

"We'll call 'em here first. Then see if we can make them run around a little." He waved the whistle. "Grab more of these if we can."

The whistle screamed into the silence — loud, breathy blasts, such as (say) a guard might emit in a life-threatening emergency. If at least some of the Alliance ran to the watchtower, we would have the advantage before they realized what had happened, as they would return in a disorganized stream, rather than being dug into their positions within the town. Dane insisted you fought best when the ground was solid under your feet, and that made sense.

As we ran for the outskirts of town, spiraling inwards, at any moment I expected to feel a crossbow bolt enter my back. What would that feel like? A punch? I had been punched before. Or would you feel the pain of the wound right away, would you feel the exact sensation of flesh parting at the impact, would it feel hot? Would I hear it before it struck, or would it be travelling too quickly?

We paused only once, so that Dane could get the gun and a glass-tipped spear out of the bundle of weapons. He handed me the spear, shoving the gun into the waistband of his shorts. I was panting, my chest heaving; I heard the swish and roar of the river still in my lungs somehow, as if it had only been waiting for this moment to surge back, not fresh water but salt, a tide returning.

Dane closed his hand around mine, hot and dry, and squeezed my knuckles on the haft of the spear till I nearly cried out: a warning, and instructions. *I can't take them all*, he'd said as we left the clearing at dawn. *You'll have to back me up*.

Take, such a word. *Take them all*: into death or at least serious wounding. But he was right. If the guards had their chance, they'd kill us, and then the survivors would have no one on the outside. Only each other, and no weapons. We at least had to get inside the building.

God, I thought. Gods, God, somebody. Manifest yourself in some form and help us. I am not saying our cause is noble. I am not saying blood has not been spilled. But help us anyway because we need help. And because since when is spilling blood a problem for you?

You'll have to back me up: that would be random chance at best. I didn't know how to build a house from looking at a completed house and I didn't know how to fight from seeing a fight. And I had not been in a fight for years, and the last time I had fought — because Reid hadn't been there to pull us apart and then kick the shit out of the other boy — it had not been with an intent to hurt him, let alone incapacitate or kill him. I just wanted him to leave me alone. I had no skill, no strategy, not like Dane. I could rely only on surprise.

And anger.

I had that now, if nothing else.

At the back entrance of the timber yard, facing the forest, stood a man and a woman — alike enough to be brother and sister, even dressed similarly in their baggy dark clothing, both armed with the simple black plastic crossbows that looked so much like the skeleton of a gun. Next to me, I felt Dane tense, his arm pressed to mine tightening, tautening, as if it too were a weapon. I had a split second to think, *What would Reid do?*

She would do whatever she had to. Cad be damned. She would fight the dogs away from me. She would drive the spear into the side of the boar.

Dane gave no signal. He simply burst from the trees, aiming directly for the woman with his spear, and for a second I felt as if I had returned to an ancestral memory: a hunter springing from ambush to kill some terrifying Paleolithic foe with our crudest weapon.

She brought her crossbow up more by reflex than anything, even managing to fire before he hit, but the bolt flew far over his head. Dane drove his spear through her ribs with a harsh grunt of effort, and they crashed to the ground; as he rolled to his feet, the spear tangled in her clothing, the other guard leapt on him, shouting for backup.

Then I was out of the trees too, not low like Dane but holding my spear at hip level, even in those last seconds trying to pretend I was doing something else — scaring off a wild dog with a stick, swatting a wasp, not attacking a human being. The man was wrestling with Dane, trying to pin him with his knees, both reaching for their knives with awkward swipes between blows, and I ran at the tangle of bodies hoping for a miracle kill.

But the man spotted me, raising an arm in surprise so that the glass tip slammed into his forearm and slid out through the cloth. He screamed breathlessly, and Dane managed to yank the knife from the man's belt and drive it upwards with both hands. Metal screeched audibly against bone.

Another two guards sprinted around the corner of the building, shouting for others in their turn, a string of unrecognizable names like casting a spell, and Dane was scrambling to his feet again, spear in one hand, knife in the other, and I resisted, again, the urge to turn and flee — my thighs trembling with the effort, knees trembling. Dane's face was bruised, his nose bloody, one wrist dangling; he threw me one last desperate look as more guards appeared: *Can you fight, will you fight?*

"It's him, the little shit!" The first of our opponents I felt I knew — yes, one of Nixon's personal guards, a tall, skinny man with fiery red hair down to his ass. Instinctively I jerked my spear downwards to try to fend him off; he evaded it easily, slapping it to one side, and punched me in the gut.

It felt like he'd impaled me with a dull piece of wood; the ground leapt to meet me, gravel clawing at the side of my face. He hammered my exposed ribs with kicks, grunting with the effort, swearing under his breath. An explosion of flames in my fingers and this time I screamed with all the breath I had left, agony shooting up my arm, his foot coming down again on my hand even though my broken fingers could no longer hold the spear. He snatched it away and paused to examine the bloodied tip, perhaps even hesitating as he recognized it to be one of his own people's weapons — and Dane rose from the dirt like a snake, catching him around the thighs, sending the spear tumbling to the ground.

Time became slow and choppy, and strangely bright; I watched the tangled movements inches from my face, man and boy, boy and man, bright red hair, blood. And then there was an opening — and I rose, snatched up the spear in my other hand, and brought it down with my full weight.

The glass snapped when it hit the ground, and I stared at it for a second, uncomprehending. Something didn't add up.

What — oh. It had gone straight through the man's throat, the soft and unresisting flesh. And out the other side. And into the gravel. Dane thrust the body away and got up, panting.

More raiders were coming, streaming out of the other buildings, in pairs and trios. Dane grabbed my shoulder, shaking me as if to wake me from sleep. "Get the doors open!" he panted. "And then do like we said! Hand out the stuff, spread out. Use the — the whistle. The codes. Go!"

I almost began to argue, but there was no time. I wanted to say *But look at all those people, you can't fight them alone* — but he was right. We had cleared this entrance for a reason. I felt nauseated from the pain in my hand, which seemed to roar so loudly I could hear it, but I forced myself to drag back the sliding door and yell something about fighting back.

The next several minutes were a blur. I didn't remember moving from the timber yard to the trees, or the trees to the town again, or what routes I had taken to return. I only knew where I was, because only one place in town so far was a bed of warm ashes.

Shivering, I took stock. My right hand was a sickening mess; just looking at it made me want to vomit, let alone the pain, huge, pulsating with every beat of my heart. Blood oozed from the broken skin at the knuckles where the bones had emerged and twisted out of place. My gut, unthinking, howled at me that I was on fire — that my hand was burning and I needed water. Instead, I took a mouthful of my shirt between my teeth and straightened out the three broken fingers with my other hand, and then waited out the darkness and the ringing in my ears till it became rushing, then hissing, then finally faded.

I rolled the swollen mess in the soft ashes till the blood clotted, and tried to if not ignore the pain, then set it aside, as I took stock of everything else. Nonstop shaking: probably not good. Should have stopped by now. Ribs intact or if broken, then not broken enough to be stabbing me in a lung when I inhaled. And I was all over in ash, head to toe, blinking it out of my smarting eyes, feeling it burn my skin and the scrapes and cuts I'd gotten, filling my ears, dyeing my clothing. Mr. Palmer's burned house concealed me in the hollow formed by the burnt-out floor, the stone foundation, and the remaining three feet of charred wood that remained in a single corner of the square structure. People rushed back and forth, yelling to each other; I could not glean any intelligence from it.

What had Dane said? The same thing we had just told the Alliance, without words: *Even if there are only two of us left to fight you, we will fight. So what do you think the rest of the townsfolk will do? They must be eliminated, not pacified, or else you will never be able to own this place the way you want.*

I opened my crusted eyes. I had no weapons with me, nothing but a way to lie with sound.

I had nothing but the Alliance came here because *they* had nothing. From us, they had taken our women and our children and anyone else who had not been killed in that first treacherous nighttime attack. From us they had taken the things we loved and would fight to protect. From *them* we could take nothing.

Even killing their people had not pulled them all into one area where we could better fight them off with our superior numbers. But they hadn't come here because they gave a shit about people. Had they. No, they wanted the other thing from us: the ability to stay in one place without dying.

Because they were dying out there. That much was clear. They couldn't feed themselves, that's why they were raiders. They couldn't hunt and they couldn't or didn't want to sit down somewhere and farm.

They wanted only to take. They wanted to take from us. Very simple. So simple you could laugh.

I ran my good hand through the ashes, seeking warm spots, seeking anything in the softness and grit: a stone, a fork, a live ember, anything that might create a spark. Fire was a weapon too, a weapon in its own right. Even before we could use it, we knew what it was, because nature occasionally used it against us. Then when we could control it, we thought that humanity was at its peak; and then we could *make* it, and we knew the world belonged to us and would never belong to anyone else ever again. Then we squeezed too hard and the world slipped out of our hands . . . but there was still and always fire.

The Alliance would kill me for this, too, but it would buy us time, it would not fail to draw the scavengers into one place; even if they were learning to ignore the false flags of our whistles, they would not ignore the fire. They would lose their heads, as we all did when things that we loved burned.

My fingertips drew something solid from the feathery ash: a scorched knifeblade, blunted but still metal. There would be stones outside. The foundation. Go on. Get up, I told myself. Get up. Get up.

I moved to my hands and knees, gingerly, aching from sitting even for the few minutes, and then the screams pulled me up the rest of the way. *Go. They might have already killed every single captive left. They're quick about these things. Unsentimental. You have to be like that. Go, go.*

I crawled free of the ash, letting it drool out of my mouth. Maybe if people saw me they would think I was a shadow, or a monster, or both; but no one noticed me at all as I crept behind the buildings, keeping close to the trees, till I reached the storeroom. Inside were voices, mingled in shouts and accusations, and I hesitated for just a moment — but no, they would not be burned, they would run out. And I would not be a murderer with intent . . . at worst I would be an accidental one and that, of course, had happened before.

No sentiment. They killed your people. This is the only way to hurt them. This is the only power you have over them: to take the only thing they consider worth defending.

I had never committed arson before; huddled against the back of the storeroom, the sparks I made from the rock and knife splashed harmlessly against the weatherbeaten wood and went out. What would I do if I were thinking clearly? I asked myself, and almost laughed. It was all so surreal, it had all gone beyond the point of nightmare and back around to some land I had never visited, where everything was backwards and upside down with its own rules.

Think, think. Make a fire first, don't just try to set the building on fire. Running out of time. Someone would see me here, a grey stone where there hadn't been one before. I scraped together a handful of leaf litter and twigs and at last that caught, the oily needles going up sullen and slow at first, then more quickly; I fed it taller and taller twigs until the exterior wood caught, then fled into the trees. *No more help. You're on your own now, little fire.*

Smoke rose in a thready line, apparently unnoticed, as the fire seemed to go out — the orange flames dying on the wood, *Goddammit*, then flickering up again, barely the size of my thumb, spreading horizontally at first and then creeping upwards towards the roof, where the flames brightened in an oddly alive way, as if they had just expressed with their body language, *Finally, something good to eat!*

I retreated farther into the brush, positioning myself behind a trunk and poking just one eye past it, seeing the world cut into two: half wood, half town. Soon the outsiders would see the smoke, must see it, and come running. And then the usual panic because they hadn't figured out how to work the well yet, and then I could slip back, find Dane again . . . the raiders would panic. I needed them to panic. I tried to squeeze it out of my own organs and send it towards them in a kind of mental pressure wave, thinking of how pure it was, how concentrated. My heart had not stopped pounding for what felt like hours. Soon, I felt sure, it would give way. But not yet, I pleaded. Not till I see if this works.

Fire fluttered across the roof tiles, and the oddly nostalgic smell of melting tar mingled with the woodsmoke. Blue at the base of it, sky-blue beneath the orange and yellow, burning much hotter. And still I leaned on my tree and tried to catch my breath and watch . . . there, the smoke billowing properly now in white clouds, and half the roof covered in an instant — seemingly a thin, even coat of flame, like paint, not eating into the shingles below.

And at last someone screamed, "Fire!"

It would not go out on its own now; it would not be like me, giving up and running away; I admired it, envied it; I felt out of my mind. I felt as if all of this was happening to someone else, the way everything in my life seemed to be happening to someone else and I was watching it from afar, perhaps from the top floor of my home (my real home, so far away, concrete that would not burn).

"Henryk!"

I turned, nearly falling — Isabel, heading a train of confused and filthy townsfolk in their sleeping clothes, all of them staring at the burning storehouse except for her. Relief flooded over me like cool water, dousing for just a moment the panic of the fire and the fight. "Come on," I croaked, hardly surprised that my voice was the barest thread, ash-choked and smoke-dried. "The woods — no, no, we're not running. There are weapons. Dane found them. Come on."

A strange sound was building, a crackling hiss, not like running water, not like weather. We moved cautiously into the trees, turning back to see a scene straight from an illustrated copy of *Paradise Lost* — the fallen angels now demons, at any rate all inhuman, on the burning lake. The sky was dark, the sun blocked by smoke, the burning storehouse all too obviously going up, and the incoherent yells of people from both sides trying to put it out. Other houses had begun to catch, and the forest around them, so dry, so much food for the flames, building into a roar like an oncoming tornado.

And layered over all of that rose the cries of pain and anger, revenge and torture, as Sprucedown struck back — the body fighting off an infection and overdoing it, the fever cooking everything, everything.

9.

My house was gone. A blackened rectangle remained, resembling its earliest days, when it existed only as a footprint marked out by my stick of charcoal, complying with town rules. Even the ash had all blown away in the firestorm, leaving the bare ground smooth and clean as the bottom of a pan. And this was what wood did, what woods did, being made of wood. I had not even considered that the fire would spread; I hadn't been thinking about that at all.

The burning storehouse (entirely gone, like my house and all its contents) had, like a plant at the end of its life, sent out seeds of sparks to be carried by the wind; and they had touched down and grown, and the breeze was just enough to fan them and not enough to put them out. About half of the town had been destroyed, mostly downwind, and a great swath of the woods too, and the tree farm. The greenhouse had not burned, but most of the panes had broken, and that was almost as bad; people would have to travel far to replace that glass. It wasn't impossible, but it would take months, and winter was weeks away. When you thought about how many people had scavenged abandoned cars in the first year after everything fell apart, then how few would have been left after the second year, then the tenth, twentieth . . . now, after sixty or seventy years, they would have to hunt as no one ever had before.

Footsteps behind me, quiet on the baked ground. I turned, and held a hand out, palm-down, offering my knuckles. Ada sniffed them, then lay down slowly at my feet, as if she were once again supervising my work, as if nothing had happened, nothing had changed. I studied what I could see of her: dusty, ashy, but apparently intact. Had she limped as she approached me? I wasn't sure; my eyes had already been blurred with tears.

I waited for the next visitor, the one who would come after his herald, and was not disappointed. Dane was limping, bandaged, and seemed to be moving through the same exhausted haze as I was. He glanced between Ada and me, raising an eyebrow, but did not call her away from my side. "Isabel's asking for you."

I didn't move. "Tell her I left. Tell her you missed me by a few minutes."

"If you're leaving, you can tell her yourself. You can do that much."

We walked past the ashes of Uncle Dex's house, reached the main road, walked down to the end. With the few surviving structures burnt mostly from the top-down, no one trusted what remained of the roofs, and until they could all be either reinforced or replaced, people were camping out.

A few of the older folks had pulled together a team to put up a couple of tipis to use as an infirmary, where the wounded could at least be comfortable and out of the weather. The skin on the outside was made out of all sorts of recovered things: clothes, tarps, blankets, curtains, odds and ends. Inside the sun made a kaleidoscope out of the patchwork, a bright mosaic travelling across the scattered patients.

Isabel's pallet was near the centre, under the open smoke flap. Uncle Dex sat cross-legged next to her on another blanket, holding a wooden cup of water, watching the old woman with a kind of focus and distance at the same time, as if he were staring both at her and through her to the ground below. His Cad had done something in the past few days, whatever it thought was a good idea, and it gave the illusion of a lace veil, his face and neck covered in tendrils of indigo, dark green, all tiny and intricate as moss, with very little unaffected skin visible between the threads. This went down, I knew, to mid-chest, and then stopped as if cut off with a knife. Dane and I had stared at it for a while, confirming it for him, turning him around to make sure before we told him; then he had shrugged and put his shirt on. What was there to do? It did what it wanted to. Among all of us on this earth it seemed to be the only thing not controlled by the whims of the divine.

I knelt next to Isabel and whispered, "It's me, it's Henryk."

Her eyes fluttered open, bloodshot and hazed, and at the motion both began to ooze tears that ran down the side of her face and into her ears. A lot of us had that now, the constant weeping as our smoke-irritated eyes tried to soothe themselves. "Water?"

Uncle Dex held the cup to her lips. I studied her anxiously as she focused on the cup; she had been stabbed, for one thing, four times, and the firestorm had swept over her retreat as it had so many others. A few of the elders had bandaged her up as best they could, but our best wasn't much. Her burns and smoke inhalation would just have to heal on their own, with all the pain and insomnia and dehydration and potential for infection that would entail.

I hated to admit that this too was part of my leaving — not wanting to stay here to watch her linger and die.

As if reading my mind, she said, "I'll be fine, Henryk." Her voice was raspy but still very much hers, and that made me feel a little better. "How's your hand?"

"Forget my hand. How do you feel?"

She smiled. "Fifty years younger. Like a warrior."

"Impressive." I took her hand gently, letting the small, cold fingers sit on my cupped palm like a fish. Dane's gaze felt like it was drilling into the back of my neck.

"Listen," she said, her voice fading by the moment; I leaned down, tilting my head to get an ear closer to her mouth. The smell of woodsmoke came off her as if I had put my head in a campfire. "This place . . . it was a good idea. It was a good effort. That's why you came, I know — that's exactly why you came. But it's *not* the way people are meant to live up here. My people, for years and years they didn't stay put like this. The land can't handle it, and it isn't meant to. We're meant to move, to follow the herds and the food and the water and the medicine — to have summer camps and winter camps and touch the land gently, gently, so it knows who we are." She paused to cough, and Uncle Dex gave her the last of the water, then got up to refill the cup.

"We used to do burns, proper ones, in the old days. Just have to remember when it's safe and when it's not, what places to burn, what the wind's doing . . . Beau said no more of that when he took over, and we had to stop. So it's been building up. The forest burning up, it didn't have to be that way. I keep telling people it's a sign. We should move — we should pick up, get on the move, properly. Maybe now people will listen to me."

"They should," I said. "You're the brains of this outfit now."

"You don't need brains to run an outfit, my darling," she murmured. "You need all the other things."

"I hope you end up with someone good," I said. "I hope you can move the way you want to move. I'm doing the same, Isabel. I'm leaving."

"Mm." She closed her eyes again; Uncle Dex dabbed at the tears on the sides of her face, running the damp cloth along her ears. "Moving north? Up the highway?"

"Yes," I said.

"Good. We'll see you there."

I hated that my last words to her were a lie, but I didn't want to tell her the truth — that I would be heading south, back home — and I also hated the truth and wanted the lie to be true. That I could not live alone and I could not live with them, and the only thing I could think to do was return to my home.

Dex and Dane walked me back to the highway, following what remained of the spiral paths out of habit; so much of the forest had burned that the town lay entirely exposed, as if a scab had been torn off. Ada had had to be physically prevented from limping behind us, and had only settled when she had been instructed to sit next to Isabel, as if she really understood what Dane was telling her. I wondered if she had. It kept striking me how odd Dane looked without the dog, subtly but constantly wrong, as if he had no shadow on a sunny day.

"Thanks for everything," I said. "And I'm sorry about what happened to the town."

"We'll rebuild," Uncle Dex said quietly.

"Isabel wants everyone to move. Not rebuild."

"We'll see," he said.

He shook my hand, and I reached out automatically to Dane, who surprised me by shaking as well.

"You did like you said," he said. "Stayed where you said you'd stay. And now you're running away."

"This is different," I said. "It's a towards. Not an away."

"How can it be a towards the place you already went away from?" he said, exasperated. "It's the same place."

"I know."

For a few seconds I entertained the wild, irrational hope that one or both of them would ask me to stay, or even offer to come with me, so that I would not travel alone, but the delusion pained me more than my broken bones and I eventually dropped my gaze. "Well," I said, "if you ever get tired of moving around, you know where to find me. They'll take you in."

I made myself walk for a count of a hundred before I turned to look back, but they were already gone.

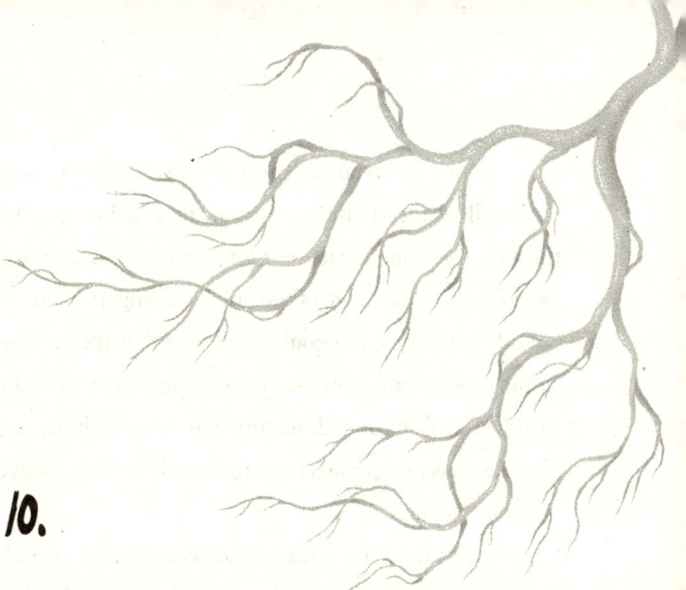

10.

Snow fell in small, sharp grains as I walked under the gate of the palisade, so that as I looked up to feel and assimilate the pain and love of seeing it again, that familiar sight, that shape like the face of a friend, the whole world seemed as if it were trying to scour it from my vision: *Don't look! Let me wipe that away!*

I stopped just inside the wall, shivering. On the journey back I had picked up more clothes not to replace but to put over my ash-stained ones, and a better-constructed rucksack made of thick plastic to replace the string bag in which I had been carrying my few remaining possessions. I did not think I looked respectable now, but I hoped I didn't look so bad I would scare the children. The first thing to do was head over to administration though, so I could see if they had reassigned my office and would perhaps give me a new one if so.

I looped both arms through my rucksack, winced at the smell of the splinted cloth on my bad hand, and headed towards the main quad — then stopped dead, and jumped quickly behind the edge of the brick building. For several heart-pounding seconds all I could think was that they had seen me coming — everyone on campus — somehow, and had massed together, joyfully united, to turn me away, kick me back out. That this was not a crowd but a mob, and a mob pointed directly at me like a gun.

It took almost a minute to realize that they weren't looking at me — that they were gathered, as they (we) (*I'm home now, aren't I? Is this real?*) often did around a central platform, and were looking at that. And I had been wildly self-absorbed or paranoid to believe that they had gathered for my sake, or maybe I had just been alone and afraid for too long; I had gotten so used to no one forgiving me for anything that I could no longer forgive myself the slightest offence. When I was done with the self-reproach, I joined the back of the crowd. The grass crunched drily under my feet, and a few people turned, glanced at me, blinked in surprise, turned back.

A hanging? A speech? What day was today — was it a holiday? I had lost track. Again I had that disorienting moment of certainty that it would be a speech about me, and how much they hated me, and that they had been doing a kind of ritual epithet desecration ceremony for the last several months, but I waited it out again and it passed.

Then a voice from the platform, coming from a face I could not see, froze me in place again with shock, with confusion, with love above all — the stunned love of the dead back to life, so that I almost shouted out loud with it.

Reid said, "Thank you, everyone who helped her. Thank you, everyone who came today. I am grateful that her pain is over."

I had heard longer speeches at funerals; I had also heard shorter. I craned my head frantically to see her, but the crowd was too thick. I began to edge around the perimeter of it, flinching as the flames began to rise, first only a heat shimmer against the lacy curtain of snow, then orange and yellow. *You, you again.* Afraid of water, afraid of fire, what else was left?

Grief had not yet struck me; I felt it in the distance, I expected and even welcomed it, but the sensation also was that it would have to get in line. I had not grieved anything the way I had wanted to for a long, long time.

Numbed, trembling, strange smells rising from the collar from my unfamiliar coat, I joined the back of the orderly queue of people waiting to hug Reid and deliver condolences or tell a story. Often this would happen for weeks here — people used to stop me in the hallways or sit next to me at dinner to say they were sorry and share a memory about my parents — because people did not want to do that at the ceremony, while the flames consumed the body hidden in its thick metal trough.

And then we were not even face-to-face but separated by three people and she saw me through the gap in winter-coated shoulders, through the light obscuring snow that was growing heavier as we stood out there, and my first thought was how terrible she looked, and my second was how terrible I must also look, because her face displayed what I felt: the shock, the love, the pity. She pushed the last few people aside and then we were embracing, tightly, my healing bones grumbling with pain as the splints pressed against her back, but I could not hold her any less tightly to me, I could not let her go.

"I'm sorry," I said. "I'm sorry, I'm sorry."

"It's okay," she said into my shoulder, the words muffled. "I knew. It wasn't a surprise."

What difference does that make, I wanted to say, but my throat closed off and I began to weep. The wind changed, bringing a gust of warm air across our faces that was almost pleasant, just for a second, it almost felt like a benison, unprayed-for and unexpected, if you didn't think about where the warmth was coming from.

Snow hissed across window like a tossed handful of sand. Reid and I sat as we had sat a thousand times, side by side on the stools at the lab bench in the room she had shared with her mother. Mrs. Graham's few possessions were spread out along the length of the bench: bags of socks and underwear, a stack of folded sweaters, a few books, a handful of enamel pins glittering like stars against the black plastic.

"I'll have to go back down pretty soon," Reid said, staring into space over my shoulder. "To get some ashes."

I nodded, studied her, waited out the pain I felt. I guess I had thought that she would be different, coming back — so there was this mismatch between the sleek, plump rabbit I thought that Howse University would have made her, and this gaunt hare with circles under her eyes so dark they looked fake, painted on. She had cut her hair short, as she sometimes did on an impulse, and what was left was too short to curl like normal. Where her hands rested on the bench, I could see every bone through the translucent skin, hiding under the marks of her Cad like pieces of wood under the river water, decorated with floating weed.

She pointed her chin at my hand. "What happened there?"

"The long version takes a while to tell," I said. "The short version is I went up north to go work with Uncle Dex."

"And then?"

"And then I came back. You?"

She laughed, short and sharp, like a bark. "I went to Howse University. And then I came back."

"I didn't expect to come back," I said. "And when I did, you were the last person I expected to see."

"Dr. G wrote me." She lifted her hand and looked at it, rubbing one thumb across the back of her knuckles so that the threads became darker and closer to the skin. "She said Mom's Cad was turning, and in her opinion it was . . . it was the last. And if I could, I should come home to see her . . ."

"Did you . . . I mean, in time?"

"Yeah." She closed her eyes and leaned her head back, and I winced to see the dark lines of the disease marching up her throat, like the marks of blood poisoning. Those hadn't been there when she left. "I got back about . . . four days ago.

I think four days. Saturday morning. So barely, barely. She passed away Monday night. I was with her. It wasn't . . ."

I gave her time to find the words. Maybe there weren't any; but she had always been better at them than I was. I thought about her application essay for Howse, the surprising keenness of it, so that afterwards I felt that I had been flayed by a blade too sharp to feel and too fine to see. But words could be stolen by grief, and that was all right too. That was not really theft. They would return.

She said, "It wasn't as bad as I was imagining. You know how sometimes it's . . . but Dr. G said that Mom probably wasn't in pain like that. She was having seizures though, all the time. At first it was just now and then, but when Dr. G wrote to me, it was a few times a day. Nonstop, nonstop. And then unconscious afterwards, but she'd wake up after an hour or so. So she knew I was there, thank God. We even managed to talk a little bit, about . . ." Reid swallowed, then shrugged, her eyes filling with tears at last. "Anyway, on Monday night she had a really bad one that lasted — it felt like forever. Honestly, it must have been eight or ten minutes, at least. And afterwards she just . . . stopped breathing." Reid wiped her face on her sleeve. "And Dr. G kind of looked at me, and I didn't know what to say. I really didn't. I had a speech and everything — it's not like I was thinking about anything else on the trip back. I just couldn't talk. Mom wasn't . . . struggling, that I could see, she wasn't . . . gasping for air, she wasn't stiff or tensed up like it hurt. I don't know.

I'll never know. And Dr. G said, 'You can say goodbye, and I'll be back,' and I . . . sat down next to the bed. And I did say goodbye."

"I . . . good. That's good. I mean, it's terrible and I'm sorry. But I'm glad you made it back. I'm glad you were with her."

"Thanks, Hen." She took a deep, shaky breath. "Me too. She wouldn't have been alone, at the end. I'm sure she wouldn't. But I'm still glad I made it in time. It was such a close thing." She studied me for a moment, just as I had studied her, and said, in a tone of light surprise and even confusion, "But how did *you* find out that Mom was dying?"

"What?"

"I . . . isn't that why you came back?"

I ran through several potential answers in my head, and finally decided on, "No."

"No?"

"No. Things went . . . very wrong. I couldn't stay there. All I could think to do was come home."

She raised an eyebrow.

I said, "I've been thinking about it, you know? I've had a good long time to think about it. Not what went wrong there, but whether it was *me*, whether it would have happened to anyone else." I picked up one of her mother's enamel pins — a lab flask and a rainbow reading *SCIENCE IS REAL!* — and put it back down. Reid watched me, waiting for me to stop fiddling. "For a while there I decided I was being punished by the gods for no reason, but then I thought maybe things happening because of the whims of a god, or fate, were still happening for a reason. And maybe my mistake was assuming that the things punishing me thought about punishment the same way I did."

"What?"

"I don't know. It was a long walk." I sighed. "If it helps, they didn't throw me out. I left. I felt like . . . I outgrew it somehow. And I was only there for a few months. Is that even possible?"

"I think so," she said. "I feel like I did the same thing."

I stared at her. "And then we . . . both came home. Is that it? Is that all? Nothing to show for it, no big fortune, we both wanted to change the world and we just gave up and *came home?*"

"No, what I mean is . . . we've been friends so long that most of the time we were the only people teaching each other how to think. Which admittedly is not the smartest way of doing things, but it's too late now. I saw how the people at Howse lived, and you saw how the people up there —"

"Sprucedown."

"Sprucedown. Okay. How they lived. And we've grown up here, so we know how *we* live. But we're all doing the same thing people did . . ." She waved her hand frustratedly. "*Back in the day.* We're ants pushing against a building. We're on the wrong track, individual people trying to change these big, heavy things that already exist, these things that people don't want to change. There's got to be a . . . a . . ."

"Fourth way? Are we up to four?"

"To live. Yeah. And it doesn't look like this, living in the skeleton of the old world that we'll never bring back to life even though that's all we can think of to do, to rebuild the old world exactly like it looked; and it doesn't look like Howse, where they pretend the skeleton doesn't exist and it's okay for people to keep dying and they made the world that the rich bunkered down into; and it doesn't look like Sprucedown, even, or you wouldn't have come home."

"No," I said, when she stopped to catch her breath. "No. Definitely not. Sprucedown is like here, and it's kind of not like here. I guess I had to see it for myself. Like, for any place to work, you've got to give people choices, and yes, that's *all* people, even people you don't like or think should be able to make choices, you have to give them real options. You can't throw a net over people to trap them and then say it's a safety net. That's two different things. You have to let people stretch and grow and do stupid stuff. The whole world can't be a net. It doesn't matter how pure your motives are."

"A real manifesto," she said. "Impressive."

"Fish traps," I said. "It's about fish traps actually."

"Anyway," she said. "Whatever the future looks like, it's something else. It's a blend of all of those things or it's a whole new thing. That's what we've got to do."

"What?"

"Sorry. Right. Getting ahead of myself. I meant: What will you do now that you're back?"

"That was very subtle," I said. "Really smooth. And I was about to say: I don't know. Find someplace to live again. Get back on the work roster again. Pretend I never left. Alternatively, it sounds like I could get drafted into your new resettlement project which seems to consist of . . . one person?"

"Two, obviously."

"A new community," I said, just to make sure I'd understood her correctly. "Of two."

"I mean not now. We've got to think about it first. Make a plan. See who wants to come."

"Why me?" I said. "I just told you I flunked out of my only experience of independent living. I don't have any qualifications for whatever crackpot ideas you're planning."

"Yes you do," she said. "You know you do."

"I'm a known quantity. That's about it."

"Sure. I know all your failure points. You know mine. But I also feel like that's what gives us the strength to do something entirely new." She brushed aside a few of the pins and reached for something hidden under a folded shirt: the boar tusk she had taken after the hunt. "We don't have anything to prove to each other. That's kind of freeing, isn't it? In terms of coming up with a plan?"

"Oh my God. It'll be like the building of St. Petersburg."

"It will not." She frowned in mock insult. "We're not going to build on a bog, first of all. Also, I was thinking —"

"Oh, no."

"— Koda started doing tattoos again. Remember how we always used to talk about getting matching ones? You and me and Nads?"

"Of course I remember."

"So you're up for it?"

"I did not say that."

She was smiling at last, a real smile under her reddened nose and eyes, and I had to smile back. "Where do you think?" she said. "Shoulder? Neck?"

"I missed you," I said. "I forget why, now, but I did."

She laughed.

H:

I meant to start writing this letter the day I got the letter inviting me to Howse. Never found a spare moment though (and I think you will agree that a lot happened sort of immediately after that). So I am writing it at 11 ish something the night before the dawn when I'm scheduled to leave. I'm holding the paper so close to my flame that it will be a miracle if I don't set it alight. One point for not procrastinating is that I would have had some daylight I guess. Lesson learned.

I am saying too much here that is meaningless. Mrs. C would yell at me for wasting paper if she knew.

Second point: I would have had time to plan what I wanted to say. I guess it is clear that what I want to say and what I will say are going to end up being very different and that's my fault for putting this off.

But here's what I am saying: it's dark. I'm scared. I feel delirious with fear, yet the enemy inside me isn't fighting. Maybe I wore it out for now. I'm afraid of the unknown, which I do (to be clear) think is a good, reasonable fear. But I'm also afraid of going into the unknown without you, my most known thing. And I'm afraid of who I might become if I never see you again.

I've sure been telling everybody how great it'll be to come back here after four years but truthfully — I can't shake the feeling — I don't think I'll be coming back. So this is all of a sudden not just a letter to say don't forget me (which I meant it to be, about a month ago), but the last thing I get to say to you. My last words, the last of my voice.

I'm not angry at you. I don't blame you for what happened. I'm proud of you for going to find your own way after I'm gone. I wish our adventures could have been together forever, because everything we are we made ourselves into, but at least we are having adventures and that's something.

Of course we are not the first young people to leave home and declare that we are going to be the ones to save the world, but I feel that we're some of the first who might actually be able to do it. And that's something too.

Almost out of paper and oil. At a later date, to be determined, crocodile.

Spread your wings. I love you.

ACKNOWLEDGEMENTS

For this final chapter of Reid and Henryk's story I'd again like to thank my infinitely loyal agent Michael Curry, and my ever-patient editor Jen Albert, who put up with a *lot* from this manuscript, my *gosh*. (Thank you, Jen!) At almost every point during the writing and editing of this book, it seemed my world was falling apart and it was my job to keep the pieces together, rather than devote time to my art. This is a book that came out of the gaps between trees, the branches between buds, the space between clouds, none of which I took the time to quantify, only feel. But I am overjoyed with the image that has arisen from these gathered scraps. Again, I would like to thank our copyeditor Rachel Ironstone and our incredible cover, created by illustrator Veronica Park and art director Jessica Albert. I would also like to thank my beloved friend Kim Scott, who has helped me for decades and most recently helped more than she knows — by gifting me the remaining tuition I needed to attend the Banff Centre Literary Arts Winter Residency in January 2024, at which the final version of this novella came together. If not for those quiet days tapping away at my laptop, looking out at the snow and the deer, this would have been a very different book. So I would also like to acknowledge the role of the Banff Centre, my mentors Waubgeshig Rice and Casey Plett, and our organizer, Derek Beaulieu. I am not sad to leave the world of these books; I am leaving with love, and perhaps one day I will return.

PHOTO CREDIT: PREMEE MOHAMED

PREMEE MOHAMED is a Nebula, World Fantasy, Ignyte, Locus, and Aurora award-winning Indo-Caribbean scientist and speculative fiction author based in Edmonton, Alberta. She has also been a finalist for the Hugo, British Fantasy, British Science Fiction, Ursula K. Le Guin, and Crawford awards. In 2024, she was the Edmonton Public Library writer-in-residence. She is the author of the *Beneath the Rising* series of novels as well as several novellas. Her short fiction has appeared in many venues, and she can be found on her website at www.premeemohamed.com.

Entertainment. Writing. Culture.

ECW is a proudly independent, Canadian-owned book publisher. We know great writing can improve people's lives, and we're passionate about sharing original, exciting, and insightful writing across genres.

Thanks for reading along!

We want our books not just to sustain our imaginations, but to help construct a healthier, more just world, and so we've become a certified B Corporation, meaning we meet a high standard of social and environmental responsibility — and we're going to keep aiming higher. We believe books can drive change, but the way we make them can too.

Being a B Corp means that the act of publishing this book should be a force for good — for the planet, for our communities, and for the people that worked to make this book. For example, everyone who worked on this book was paid at least a living wage. You can learn more at the Ontario Living Wage Network.

This book is also available as a Global Certified Accessible™ (GCA) ebook. ECW Press's ebooks are screen reader friendly and are built to meet the needs of those who are unable to read standard print due to blindness, low vision, dyslexia, or a physical disability.

The interior of this book is printed on Sustana EnviroBook™, which is made from 100% recycled fibres and processed chlorine-free.

FSC
www.fsc.org
MIX
Paper | Supporting responsible forestry
FSC® C016245

ECW's office is situated on land that was the traditional territory of many nations, including the Wendat, the Anishinaabeg, Haudenosaunee, Chippewa, Métis, and current treaty holders the Mississaugas of the Credit. In the 1880s, the land was developed as part of a growing community around St. Matthew's Anglican and other churches. Starting in the 1950s, our neighbourhood was transformed by immigrants fleeing the Vietnam War and Chinese Canadians dispossessed by the building of Nathan Phillips Square and the subsequent rise in real estate value in other Chinatowns. We are grateful to those who cared for the land before us and are proud to be working amidst this mix of cultures.

ecwpress.com